THE BISMUTH QUEST

Possum Burton

For my family.

Foreword

Hullo. This book is a tale of adventure, coarseness and scientific endeavour. Alas, all three of those things can prove rather shaky, at least on the surface. You might need to rotate your book a bit in order to fully understand this modest tale, such as it is. I hope you enjoy reading it and I wish that its characters become your acquaintances.

Best of best wishes, with mandolin and cello,

Possum Burton, 6 August 2025

The Players:

PROFESSOR WOODY REDWOOD, *boffin*

DAGMAR JAKESPEARE, *boffin*

EDGAR HALBERD & CHIX BABBELL, *intendeds*

TYRAN HALBERD, *Edgar's father, landowner*

ORFEUS HOPP, *author and sculptor*

Setting: The southern half of the Lylas Isles, 2020s. Also mystical times. With elves!

Anyway, wooing. Woody wants to build a centre. In Kerno. For research. KERN. Bringing together all the physical laws that are independent of emotion. Ah. $F = Gm_1m_2/r^2$, G is summat of the order -11, but what of its units? Qui peut dire. Dirac! Dirac that brilliant scientist. Woody, OTOH, is just a nerd. He wants some bismuth for a wedding gift – Chix and Edgar both love metals – but where to get it?

Arguments were a constant diameter between Woody and Dagmar. Both attempting to be as nice as they could be. Very scary gauge bosons. Fatiguing. Professor Woody Redwood is a Welwyn Garden City hardman. He doesn't make ideal threats. Mathematical ideals! Algebra! A quirky geezer. "Finnegans Wake" is a good book but it smells of biscuits. Woody is Irish but *Finnegans Wake* is just too Irish. He will kneel before Chapelizod, howevs. With gaminess.

Woody loved mathematics. It was his lazaretto, his religious ecstasy, his perfumed paradise. He summed his way out of the grimy clay that immured him. Once, while musicking with Dagmar, he imagined the wave equation undulating in the air. Oo err. Were Sheela-na-gigs real? All this was pretty embarrassing, but sometimes embarrassing things have to be written. What's bismuth? Woody must find it else she dies. Stuck Woody will find it hard to put aside his ambitions! He's given himself the task of subduing the wokers. Woke's not Woody's thang. Woody, like Dagmar and Orfeus, regrets everything a small amount.

-The next part will be upside down. Soz!!!!!!!-

Weddings! They're not really that bad, but Woody has to make a point of them. Fortitude. Courage! The gubbins of clothes. Woody has clothed goblins. The countryside is ardently brown. Not at the cul-de-sac of history. Woody's trying to learn the liturgy of marriage. He needs a gift.

He needs a new planet wherein to store all the things he's learned. Strength beyond grumbles. Stuff has been mounted up. The action is present. He is here, angular. Graphs. Geometries. Roots. Alphas and betas. Woody can play the part of an impish impresario; Val's prepped him up. Woody's a bit like Osiris's lost bits. Scattered across a desert. Neologisms become datedisms, Val points out. Monies. Bandana on. *Phantom Pain* t-shirt on. As an aside, Woody remembers the controversy: trebuchets of insults ready to launch. It was like the ship stuff in *Assassin's Creed III* and *IV* … Assa… assa… assas... Take the baptism of death… assisted death. Old words in new mouths… The nation works… Sinister things defeated in a peaceful scrap… the small font withdraws. Knowledge – kennings – tightened like a screw. Lots and lots of examples. The tower rises. Volumes, eh? Against time travel. Decibels. Woody wears loose t-shirts. Precision needed, after war. Sharp and magical. Woody surfs over tyrannic silence. You'll find G*d and the D*vil in silence. Misplaced foreboding… Wickedness daily. Wasn't this book about a wedding gift?!

Back to KERN. A physical centre. A paean to science and love.

Would be nice to experience the latter. You already have, Woody.

You could do summat about bismuth, says Dagmar. She's icing.

Bi? says Woody. What a boring element. I know nowt about it.

Chillax, replies Dagmar. Play the guitar. Get a 3 week turnaround.

Tidy up. Dust.

*-e-i\ Not panicking during a presentation. Please read these pages in any order. Woody's thinking about a curry menu at present. o+o¡

The devil's fulcrum bounces on. What has this to do with a tying of the knot? Val tidied the pub a bit on his way back from his trip outside to use the hedge facilities. Chix, that lass, knows some capoeira moves. A fine capoeirista. Acquired martial arts skills. She's also a generous livestreamer.

It's a goofy wedding. Edgar is as laid back as an autumnal maple leaf on a pond. Err of the chillaxers. Chill pills. Val loves metals. Woody archives. The crowds return. Don't become resentful. Be foetusesque your whole life. Teamwork like Los Alamos. Los Welwynsita. Briefer than a microsecond, vita. Good and evil tussle in you every second. Val reads a James Herbert novel. Then he returns, digressively, to the bar. The humans of his country are becoming slaves again, animals!!! I am not a zoo-man, said Woody. He is trying to help the archipelago's residents, even the peninsularists.

Woody's a complete badman, like a Classical villain. Woody doffs his cap to the Yanks. Manage resentments. Beautiful shades of grey. He knows a sound opened up in WGC in 2099. Redwood's a med sci- with a strong heart. Bit self-important. The wedding. Confetti-and-bouquet time.

What are the aerodynamix of the wedding? Who's getting flown? Confetti flung. Val went up to the bar and ordered another cyder. Woody thought about the institution of marriage. Never married was he, alas, and prematurely ag^{1}ed. Ah well. He had his chums and his detective novels. But he was presently scared: the wedding! Different births, seemingly. More moving parts than the Peninsular War.

Rain drizzled outside. Woody grumbled a bit about sandwiches. Val sat on him.

-The wedding!

"It's all compacted evasion," purred Val. "Calm it lovey (Woody)".

Woody's on a fructifying journey. He's got a batch of pancakes. The wedding. Did we die? Mental tempests. Woody's saying nowt. The nuptials. Woody's baking bread that will rise later. Dance in red.

Dagmar's doing video game translations. A grey, frustrating age. All v. simbolik. Woody alone, outcast. Aloof. Vituperative. Sorry. Solid lands. It's all a routine. Who are the next targets? Who? Trees... Will it all be a petulant tantrum? Mossy querci. Otters somewhere. Orfeus somewhere. Orfeus has s gone loco. Misery loves company, apparently. The year is MML. The nuptials. Val trots off to the shops to get supplies. Clothes for the wedding. The creeping night had turned to day. Appearances is bodies. Lord's wiv 'em. Mysticism?

Anyway. Vacuum in the country. It's not what I prioritise, said

Val. General air of delirium. Woody ran his hands through the dark

wood of his hair. The wedding. The wedding. And the bismuth.

Woody knew Chix and Edgar weren't sniffy about bismuth.

Val went up to the bar and bought a cheap shandy for Woody.

"Get this down you right now, rn," said the loyal dog to his man.

-Thanks, hound. Don't sweat. My consciousness is sojourning rn.

"The wedding," prompted Val. Woody sighed and thought about

it.

-The thing's a hirsute wendigo of a problem. I'm getting #:ee[]...

Woody noticed an old painting on the wall from 2044. Woody

stared at the brushwork – a Vivienne Calloway – while the hound

sipped his dram. Val will only sip the finest rum. His narrow ears perk up with pleasure. A messy success on the fruit machine had taken place. Coins tumbled like shot birds. Wealth is a sharp onion.

Woody overheard a punter insult his (the punter's) wife. Oi, mate, said Woody, don't talk to your woman like that. That is proper narsty. Soört it awht, please. The chillaxed man has an advantage in 2100.

All right, mate, said the punter, --, and apologised to his grateful missus. Reading Proust on a sunlounger, not Hawthorne or Twain.

Reminds me of school, muttered Woody to Val. I didn't tell Dagmar about everything that went on in my schooldays, because I was too redfaced for my teachers. Blumming beaks. *Thunderbolt* readers. Val nodded in understanding as Woody seamlessly went onto the subject of footie.

Sundry, lòtsa, mess. Empathy, innit. Friendly projectiles. 5-0. Mega.

The canine liked conjunctions. Formal clothes pleased him and he had a snout for justice. Wuff-wuff-wuvee. 2011-2014 had been an arid time. Absolutely nowt. Val doesn't complain about his life; he still has one. Comfortable jumpers. Pat owns a masculine dark coat. Woody's are stressful and can make your cabeza explode. The wedding. Acquiring gifts. The wedding. The wedding! The past is just different, y'no, concluded Val. The young whippet will wag his tail.

A ditty. Poetry. Woody's plans. Years. The wedding. Unspecified +ve emotions. Reports from 2019. A strong yr of righteous memes.

Dagmar has to put out the bins like a swaggering hardwoman. Can't show weakness. She's a beautiful woman. How did Germany lose the First World War? That vexed exam question. Dagmar didn't know how to answer that. She's a tease, not a belittler. What leaf is this on?

Sunday roast, no gravy! Good listening, no escape. Having all the books in the world. Dagmar loves collecting the papery fellas. Trees are no longer a rarity in Briten. Woody has dreamt of becoming a fisherman, like ORFEUS or John. Dagmar's persistent but she doesn't want to become a fixed part of a talking shop. The Victorian haze is a capacitor of beautiful literary charge. Lots of abrasive books tho'. Ah well.

Val foresaw a meteorite landing on St Michael's Mount, during an Indian summer. Might that ferocious space rock contain bismuth?

Dagmar is making a cute sculpture in the shape of free speech.

Cosmetic? Greedy? Desperate? As Manichean as a sheer cliff face.

…The whole world's not a North London derby, Val reflected.

Dagmar went carousing under the early evening light, wearing a nice comfy green jumper! Dagmar likes Hallowe'en, but she doesn't celebrate it. Mytholmroyd the cat passes by in a crimson hoodie. Evening, says the cat. Right, lovey, says Dagmar. The evening went on. The cat's head got bigger and grander, as a way of scaring the luminescent choughs. Effulgent sparrows spoke leading questions. Mytholmroyd went back to his house and did some hoovering and then he thanked his humans for being neat and active houseguests and then Mytholmroyd dozed off and dreamt of his deceased rival.

Dagmar notices the odd odd things. Odd can be so sinister

A battered cod appeared for Woody and Val's construction. Yum! Food is pretty and necessary. Val is plumping up under the grub of Pisces. Nomworthy.

Val got out his moby from his backpack and videocalled Orfeus, who was at that moment sunning himself on the technetium promenade in Hatfield. When does Woody read the *Clerk's Tale*?

"How's the woofs?" asked Val.

-Pretty swell, bro. Nice ice creams. How's the human? (Orfeus spoke with a thick marsupial accent).

"Asleep nah. Bit chatty. How r u, little brother? … I won't call you that."

-Toasty. As warm as Vesta. I'm enjoying seeing and hearing the Heortfordshire sights. But it's too immediate for me to say much.

"I thought Heortfordshire resembled *Carnival of Souls*."

-No, that's the creepy old cinema in Tetra, or the Welly-G waxwork museum in Ruthbedh. I'm sincere about all this, not a being a sly bug.

Val put some harmless cosmetic powder on his face. Gotta keep up appearances. Howls must.

"What do you think of the engineering in…"

-Poor. Spinning awkwardly. Do you remember the equations of angular motion?

"How could I forget? Degrees of magnetism, were they? No, nein."

Val and Orfeus torqued a bit more. Woody snored. The pub's ceiling turned into flowers. Maps appeared on the walls. Woody awoke and donned his fave verdant trousers with showy, grumpy difficulty. THE WEDDING. The wedding flew through the professor's mind like a spooky galleon. He is wrecked. 2 much booze. Woody is rude $^\circ_\circ{}^\circ$ unfinished. He'll get there. What is he trying to do?

"Governments must be engaged and unbeholden to historical models." – R. Y. Cleeve. Capital letters. Audience moving on.

The venue. Woody must find a venue for Chix and Edgar's shindig. No, not a venue. A gift.

What endures after the chemical reaction? What is precipitated? Bismuth. Pure bismuth. Bi.

Is this Anglo-Saxon roleplay, asked Woody.

No, returned Dagmar, lovingly. Dagmar's favourite colour is purple. The orange sun continued. It's not a scary time. Dagmar wears pink shorts. It's 19:24. Woody puts a Carly Crooner doublesider on the record player... Irregular sound. Don't want no patronising hornswoggle. Dagmar's always jokin'. Is she doing right? Is she a good mistress? Is she leaving a good and gold legacy? Dagmar studied a piece of nankeen cloth at 20:00. The lady carries a music centre with her and mandolins are unsurprisingly given a dominant position. Right now, at 21:30, clamminess was gone, kaputt! New myths were not needed; the strong whippets, Pat and Val, were OK (<3 <3).

The wedding! Marriage deals. Ranks. Val has another scene with Woody:

Woody: Have you heard about Stevie Samson?

Val: "Yes. He's bought a new bookshop in Lincoln Street and dug a new swimming pool."

-Lincoln Street, did you say?

"Yes, Lincoln, as in "Lincoln Bomber".

-There's a wonderful cathedral in Lincoln.

"Yes, yes. Yep. (.)"

{(.) means there's a pause}

Somewhere, on the moon Miranda, Dagmar was in the act of rehoming an English dictionary. Words for days, there. Soundclips clicked and spoke with fluency. At the dinner, talking with Edgar,

Woody munched a mountain of tasty mince. Lasagne. Food made collars bearable. Woody's trying to plan a wedding. It's a grand whale of a thing. Lots of stress. Instress? Scrawled numbers – thinks of pasties.

**

Chix & Edgar are at the point of strappin' on the ball-and-chain. Woody thinks of Dagmar, who is the castle of a woman he has to protect, because manliness. Back to wedding planning. Woody was hunting Nero and Caligula and Caracalla. Back to the wedding. Gorge and vulnerability doing a thousand. Vomiting and pressure. Weddings are often stressful. Did Woody hate Chix and Edgar? Why were they in the same book as fiends? Chaos. Chao I and Chao II are fiends, aren't they? Woody listens to beauty. Long dead, isn't it? Woody put hair granules in his hair.

Anyway, sickness. That's a theme. The book = the experience made Woody ill. Sickness and time waxing and waning. Making the world a better place. Repeating a paragraph by mistake. Hayfever. Acquiring the berry of resilience. Slowly slowly. The mayfly of beauty can be tainted. Long bridges can collapse, under their weight, on Mars. Unreadable, delirious tosh. Essay at the end for a laugh. A chortle, perhaps. Writing out by hand. Yoooooofh! Black rain, quite dull. Woody is waiting in Tlaloc's Inn 4 sum1. Some books will age well, some will not. Arr. Yarr. Style bulges, exploding like a filled suitcase. Cool water on rocks. Going for a sleep now. *Post scriptum* living roughly atm. Woody in the middle. Safe island. Whippet, sleepy dreamer and I. Four hours of metre. Woody doesn't have to give a view on *TZ*.

! ! !

An attempt. Republish. Hoping on a fruitful summer. An empty summer. A clean break. The wedding! A new one. Completely new.

Reissuing old ones. prices yoked well. For delectation. Best 20th century novel. Making the most of a spurt. Preparing. Woody talks to Val, a whippet; Val responds at length. EXPERIENCE. Not woke.

"What you have to do, Professor," said Val, "is, … or well, be, to verbally reference a tiresome experiment – like adverbs – is move towards a success. The wedding's a success if people like it, not because it makes you a lot of money. Let me finish. My time is as precious as emeralds, and so is yours. Bar. Bûr. I shall not wrench my canine rhythms. I am a boffin of good. I bark in twos. R is resistance. My strong feet have a small area. You might rant under the sun. I might not starve digitally. I'd rather not. Who are you, Professor Woody Redwood, you grump? Your happiness cannot be spoken; you have no tail to wag. I love you and I climb on top of you. There there: I, Val, am here 4u."

To further the impact of her novel and its themes on the reader, Charlotte Brontë employed a variety of literary techniques, both literal and figurative in *Jane Eyre* in order to evoke sympathy in the reader, either towards Jane or towards Brontë's opinions and social beliefs. (Conjecture as no-one can travel back in time to interview Brontë). Many of these techniques, such as pathetic fallacy, whilst perhaps profound in Brontë's time, feel clichéd and ineffective in the twentieth century. However, some remain potent and affecting, albeit not always for their original meaning. Moreover, the full effect of a heavy use of religious references and metaphors is largely lost on a twenty-first century reader. The effectiveness of Brontë's use of more literal techniques, such as the bildungsroman structure in evoking sympathy is also variable. Sometimes it works very effectively, and other times it makes Jane appear a frustrating character to the reader.

The entire novel is told in the first-person narrative, Jane Eyre's point of view. One of the reasons that Brontë uses this narrative voice is because it creates a strong empathic connexion between the reader and the protagonist. This connexion leads to greater sympathy in the reader when Jane is bullied. At Gateshead, 'the blood from my head trickling down my neck' and the fact that 'every nerve I had feared John (Reed)' give very precise details of Jane's suffering to the reader. The lexical choice 'trickling' implies a slow psychological torture that carefully eats its way into Jane's thoughts, until every nerve she has fears John. The effect of such bullying, physical and psychological on a small child may have been more shocking to a Victorian audience than it is now, because in the twenty-first century such brutality appears more often in the media than it did in Brontë's time. Many of those who could read at Brontë's time were middle- to upper-class, and so may have been largely desensitized to the hardships of contemporary living for many people in that time. Therefore, to read about the cruel bullying the young Jane receives may have appeared especially shocking and unexpected to Victorian readers. Even so, the harsh treatment of an innocent child is still found cruel and appalling by readers in 2010, because inflicting such hardship on a child is still considered wrong.

The structure of bildungsroman is used constantly throughout the novel to track Jane's growing social, political and psychological development as she grows older. Jane constantly faces challenges throughout the novel, and must formulate responses to these difficulties. Both Jane's suffering and her answers to it evoke sympathy in the reader with her character. At the beginning of the novel, the reader sides with Jane over the 'wicked and cruel boy' who bullies her, because Jane is a friendless and excluded orphan. On the other hand, in the Victorian era there would have been some readers, upper-class like the Reeds, who would not have understood Jane's protestations against her treatment, instead believing them to be 'part of life' due to her being a classless orphan. They may even have thought that a poor orphan like Jane should be sent to the workhouse, instead of living in a grand manor. Nowadays, the rigid beliefs of the class system are seemingly less widely held, and so the vast majority of readers will take Jane's part against John and the other antagonists at Gateshead. However, had Jane exhibited such violence when she was an adult, the reader's sympathies would not have been with her, because that would have meant she had not matured. The child Jane's attack on John was understandable, because Jane is a young child, yet such violence would not be permissible when the adult Jane returns to her oppressor Mrs. Reed. It would show a lack of development and maturation in Jane's character. Therefore, audiences would not sympathise with a character that has so much long-standing hate in them. This would evoke little sympathy in the reader with Jane's character. In actuality, Jane forgives Mrs. Reed with extraordinary maturity, even though Reed reveals that Jane's large would-be inheritance was kept from her out of spite. Jane gives Reed her 'full and free forgiveness', which considering all the wrongs done to her, is truly admirable to both readers past and present. Jane even manages to feel sorry for this 'poor suffering woman'. To some readers, particularly those living in modern times, such a lack of animosity in Jane would be frustrating. These readers may feel that Jane needs to exact some sort of revenge on those who have been so cruel to her, but most readers would not agree with this interpretation. To many audiences, especially Christian Victorian ones, forgiving others is extremely important. It shows a mindset in Jane which is far more grown-up than that of her former enemies. Brontë's use of the bildungsroman structure is excellent, because it evokes great sympathy for Jane both as an adult and a child, although the maturation in attitude that Jane goes through over the course of her life may cause feelings of irritation in some readers due to her lack of vitriol towards her oppressors. What does this have to do with Woody Redwood and his search for a bismuth wedding gift?

Brontë uses pathetic fallacy in the novel to foreshadow bleak future events for Jane in order to evoke sympathy for the heroine in the reader. For example, on the night Jane accepts Rochester's marriage proposal, the tree he proposed under is 'struck by lightning... and half of it split away'. The tree's cleaving in two indicates that Jane and Rochester will soon be pulled apart by some drama. The lexical choice of 'split', both a verb causing a complete separation and a noun referring to the end of a relationship, foreshadows this. This writing creates some unease in the reader concerning Jane's fate and so the reader sympathises with her. Audiences past and present would understand that Rochester and Jane are to be parted, but Victorian audiences would likely have noted the religious connotations of the splitting of the tree. This is because in Christian belief, marriage makes the man and woman one flesh, which can only be separated by death or divorce. The death or the divorce of Rochester would naturally affect Jane, especially as the divorce would imply Rochester's infidelity (this being the only credible grounds for divorce in Brontë's time). Due to Brontë's contemporaries being more religious than now, the implication of Rochester being an adulterer would evoke more sympathy in the reader than now, because although to a modern audience adultery is still wrong, in the Victorian times it had a far greater stigma due to the Christian belief that it was a sin.

The religious symbolism of the horse chestnut splitting would largely be lost on a twenty-first century secular audience, although they would still understand the foreshadowed hint of hardship for Jane. However, by 2010 the effectiveness of this event is somewhat lost due to similar metaphors for the separation of lovers being in common use in the arts, including in art forms that did not exist in Brontë's day. This makes this use of pathetic fallacy feel trite and unoriginal to the reader. The tree splitting was probably not that clichéd to the Victorian reader, as few books with featuring such metaphors had been written before. In conclusion, the cleaving of the chestnut tree would have evoked much sympathy with Jane in 1850; as such pathetic fallacy would have been new and original. However, to a twenty-first century reader this literary technique appears unoriginal and dull.

Religious lexis is used by Brontë to paint Mr Brocklehurst as a satanic character. Brocklehurst demands that a girl's naturally curling hair should be cut off, because he believes 'we are not to conform to nature'. To a Christian audience this statement is very powerful and shocking, because according to Christian belief everything in nature was made by God, and anything not in nature would have been made by the devil. Brocklehurst is therefore demanding people exist in a manner which exults the unnatural and therefore the satanic. This would increase the religious reader's fears for Jane, because she is under the control of a character figuratively implied to be a devil worshipper. To a secular audience however, this comparison with the devil is nowhere near as strong. Brocklehurst's worldview is a cold one ungrounded in reality. He is a delusional fantasist.

There are many other, non-religious interpretations of this 'not to conform to nature' lexis. One is that it is an attempt to promote sympathy for the feminist cause. Brocklehurst makes his remarks after a girl's hair is too garish for his puritan liking. This could be a metaphor for the oppression women of Brontë's time felt under the male-dominated hierarchy. The girl cannot express her full femininity – her hair – because of men (e.g. Brocklehurst) decide for her how to act, dress and so on. Brontë, a known feminist, is passing judgement on the societal treatment of women at the times and of the segregation that men imposed upon them. In addition to the religious lexis mentioned earlier, this was probably one of Brontë's main motivations when writing this line.

An alternative interpretation of Brocklehurst's 'not to conform to nature' statement is that it is an attack on the unjust class system of Brontë's time. By nature, everyone is born equal, but people do not live their lives as such. Brocklehurst himself is an example. He encourages his charge to live as paupers, because he feels this is his task from God, yet his daughter is amazed that the students look on her 'as if they had never seen a silk gown before'. Brocklehurst's family are clearly far better off than the children in his school. This quote shows how separated society was and is and the lack of communication between the rich and poor. There are those who by no work of their own have privilege, whilst others no biologically different from them do not. This message would have been very powerful in Brontë's time, and only marginally less today. This is because in 2010 there are still those with plenty of wealth and those with none, and this is due to factors not found in nature, such as class and money. (Some animals are weaker than other animals of the same species, but whether these differences constitute classes is anyone's guess).

This quote could also work on a biological level. Brontë's message could be that females are one half of nature, and should be treated like males. Theoretically, men and women should be treated equally, thereby 'conforming to nature'. However this doesn't happen. For example, the men do not have to style their hair a certain way, so why should the women? This message of equality is one the feminist Brontë would likely have propagated. Because Brontë's metaphor is about the stifling of a perfectly natural property, great sympathy with the feminist cause is evoked by pro-women apologists both in her time and in the present day. Due to the social beliefs Brontë was protesting against this message would have been largely ineffective in the time of *Jane Eyre*'s original publication. However, due to an upsurge in feminism and less rigid social beliefs, the message is more resonant and affecting in 2010, and so more likely to evoke sympathy with the poor treatment of women at Brontë's time.

Satanic imagery is used to deprecate Jane and so create sympathy with her in the reader. At Thornfield, Adèle discovers three self portraits Jane painted at Lowood, one of which is 'crowned with a

16

star'. To a Victorian audience the wearing of a star would be associated with devil worship and Lucifer. This is clear self-deprecation from Jane, showing her huge lack of self-esteem. Normally, comparing oneself with the devil is such a huge self-insult that it implies that one is simply fishing for compliments. However, Jane painted these at Lowood, when it was under the cruel auspices of Brocklehurst, who constantly told her that she was 'vile', 'a liar', and destined for 'an awfully sudden death'. This would have had a huge influence on the child Jane, and her childish naivety means that it is highly likely that she would have believed herself to be diabolic. This comes across in her portrait, and so huge sympathy is created in the reader both past and present with Jane's lack of self-worth, slightly more so in Victorian times as beliefs in the pure evil of the devil were more firmly entrenched.

An alternative interpretation of this self-deprecating language is that it is an attempt to evoke sympathy for the feminist cause. Jane refers to this painting as a 'vision of the Evening Star'. The Evening Star, a cosmological object, often has connotations of the devil, because the Evening Star's apparent descent from the sky after sunset is supposed to represent Lucifer's fall from heaven. The Evening Star is actually the planet Venus, which has always been considered female. Therefore Jane is comparing the very emblem of womanhood to the devil. This satanic deprecation of women is indicative of what many women actually felt at Brontë's time. Brontë's message is that evil connotations have been placed onto Venus – and therefore women – with no justification. This is a powerful message, especially to people in the present day, who have been less influenced by the gender stereotypes of Brontë's time and feel that less of a stigma and fewer stereotypes need to be attached to being a woman.

I believe these two interpretations are not mutually exclusive. Brontë can use this imagery to get across the low self-esteem of her protagonist and also spread her views on the injustices of Victorian society. Although an engaging coming-of-age story with flashes of romance and Gothic horror, *Jane Eyre* is more of a social critique than a novel. Through Jane the reader experiences many of the cruelties of mid-Victorian society, such as the almost insane arrogance of the Reed family as they treat Jane in a most disgusting way. Other contemporary societal problems explored in the novel, besides others include immorality, especially of a sexual nature (Rochester's adultery), religious fanaticism, stifling misogyny and the gaping chasm between rich and poor. An objective reading of *Jane Eyre* can still be achieved, although the societal themes within will definitely permeate the mind of the reader to a large extent. The Brontës were a bit intense. They were from Yorkshire, after all...

To conclude, *Jane Eyre* is still an entertaining novel, pretty front row, truth be told, but many of the ideas and themes in it have not aged well and are largely irrelevant to the modern day, such as the religious iconography. The way people are devoted to video games these days is similar to how they once would have been devoted to religion. However, the myriad flaws of a largely uncaring capitalist society still resonate strongly today. Likewise, some aspects of Brontë's metaphorical writing are still relevant today, albeit for reasons different to those Brontë intended. The general idea of bildungsroman is still effective. Jane's many actions throughout the book show her development into a good human being and therefore, despite many faults, in the writing and Jane's character, Jane is still a character towards whom readers can feel great sympathy. She's presented as a sensitive and discerning woman. On occasion, Brontë's techniques can be devastatingly effective and her messages vividly expressed.

***

Let Mytholmroyd the cat enter this story. Myth, as it shall be convenient to refer to him, dozes a bit in Woody and Dagmar's hexagonal flat.

Mytholmroyd, Mytholmroyd

Mytholmroyd, Mytholmroyd purrs at night
Because he wants another bite
"Some more brown biscuits and some fish,
"That's what I want, humans, that's my wish."

Yet fit and limber as great athletes be he,
He squeezes between humans when he climbs the settee,
Solidly built like an Olympian swimmer;
On silvery mornings his robes of fur glimmer.

What a grand feline! What a great mane!
When his owners are out the flat's his domain;
But in the evening light, when he hears a carriage return
He graciously cheers the return of Woody and Dag-mur.

Not a fat cat, not a bully
His bountiful fur is fluffy, not woolly.
What a lion! What a pose,
What a radiant creature lives and strolls!

Playing TV snooker, potting the balls,
In the nature documentaries Africa calls
To an acute-eyed feline with Elizabethan ruff;
Who knew lazing all day could make one so tough?

Mytholmroyd, Mytholmroyd purrs at night
Because he wants another bite
"Some more brown biscuits and some fish,

"That's what I'd like, humans, that's my wish."

Electromagnetics – how do you say 'Biot-Savart'?

Electromagnetic doorbells are an example of a self-interrupting electrical circuit. A step-down transformer will typically reduce the house's 110—120-volt current to the 10 to 18 volts at which doorbells and chimes operate. When the bell push is pressed the switch inside the circuit is moved to the on-position. This completes the circuit such that an electric current will start to flow from the battery through the circuit. The flow of this current through the coil will generate a magnetic field around the wire perpendicular to the current, magnetising the coil. This current will flow through the coil of wire wrapped around the soft iron core. This iron core has been annealed so that it has a low-carbon content and can hence be magnetised and demagnetised with little fatigue. The presence of the iron core increases the strength of the electromagnet [the coil of wire] as it concentrates the magnetic field lines. This has the effect of greatly strengthening the magnetic field around the coil. The magnetic field strength and magnetic flux density thus both increase. The armature [a small rod of iron connected to a spring] is therefore attracted to the coil and moves towards it quickly. This motion causes the small metal hammer at the end of the armature to strike a gong beneath the circuit, but the movement of this hammer creates a gap in the circuit. This break in the circuit causes the magnetic field to collapse, so the armature springs back to its initial position. In so doing it remakes the circuit and the current flows once more through the coil to attract the armature and the gong is struck again. This process repeats and so the gong is repeatedly struck.

****

&/:if_commandDante,   &/:if_commandDante,

&/:if_commandDante,

Cornish? English? The year is 700. Where do the Vikings fit in? And the dragons?

Where do your cleaning skills fit in, Woody snapped at Dagmar.

You weak man, she snapped back, cloth in hand.

*

Have you ever read anything by Flannery O'Connor, Dagmar asked Woody.

No. Too American.

*

Karitas

Charity shop, 2039 – 2041. Dagmar is the new volunteer.

Titles: 2018-2024 [Scotland]

The Vampire of Falmouth

The Mummy of St Michael's Mount

Witches of Welly-g (the lower gravity in that place allows for flying)

Demons of Norwich – Furies on the Roof!!!

The Dragonfly of Santorini will Perturb and Sustain you

Elves at the Eden Project

2034: Ghoul-faced Kingo

2035: Dagmar's Career

The narrator's head is bursting with ideas, says Woody. It's like an explosion in a deep-sea trench.

Maybe we should start at the beginning, said Dagmar. In the year 2050. Let's hazard our ease. Let's go back. Back to that funfair.

{General games and carousing. Edgar plays the pianoforte.}

DAGMAR

(through a loud hailer)

WE ARE LOOKING FOR BISMUTH.

Woody: We commence with linear algebra. What is a basis? What is linear independence? What's a standard basis? I've got a blue highlighter.

Dagmar cut in at this point, so early on in the novel, to say that this was too much maths.

WOODY

It is not. Stay focused, young lady.

Dagmar apologised for her complaint. She lazily drew old equations on her pad with a black pen, jocose old friends from the lake of Lethe:

$$a^2 + b^2 = c^2$$

$$(x + a)^n = \sum_{k=0}^{n} \binom{n}{k} x^k a^{n-k}$$

$$A = \pi r^2$$

$$(1 + x)^n = 1 + \frac{nx}{1!} + \frac{n(n-1)x^2}{2!} + \ldots$$

$$x = \frac{-b \pm \sqrt{b^2 - 4ac}}{2a}$$

$$f(x) = a_0 + \sum_{n=1}^{\infty} \left(a_n \cos\frac{n\pi x}{L} + b_n \sin\frac{n\pi x}{L} \right)$$

$$e^x = 1 + \frac{x}{1!} + \frac{x^2}{2!} + \frac{x^3}{3!} + \ldots, \qquad -\infty < x < \infty$$

$$\cos\alpha + \cos\beta = 2 \cos\frac{1}{2}(\alpha + \beta) \cos\frac{1}{2}(\alpha - \beta)$$

$$\sin\alpha \pm \sin\beta = 2 \sin\frac{1}{2}(\alpha \pm \beta) \cos\frac{1}{2}(\alpha \mp \beta)$$

Dagmar opened her loved and foxed book of fairy tales and began to read.

"The darkness is present. Dagmar seems to be a constrained woman, trapped in a hollow parallelepiped of ashen edges. She's not really a happy woman. She wears neutral shades like yellow, green and red and she has to amuse herself. Realistic imagination is never far from hand and is inside each of us."

Woody, for once, understood. He used to sleep on the floor as well, on an old sleeping bag, frightened of dying during his sleep or of not being able to fall into sleep. Nowadays he sleeps easily in his hut, but he never lies in.

Moscow, 7 January ¬

Dear Professor,

Just a little card to tell you that my holidays are going fantastically, like a smooth motion picture. I'm writing to you in a beautiful café on the corner of Red Square not far from my hotel – impressive, I must say. The weather is much better here than I was expecting and I'm finding Moscow to be a really beautiful city full of all sorts of attractions. You must visit soon! There are certainly a few gardens here but you will find a veritable feast for your eyes all the same.

Today I went to the Kremlin and fell completely in love with it. The architecture is magnificent and the scale incredible. You would love this place as well, I am sure. What's more, a very kind tourist lady agreed to take several photos of me in front of the fortress. I'm going to send you them as soon as possible, as well as this letter.

Yesterday I took myself off to the Bolshoi Theatre and Saint Basil's Cathedral, they are both excellent and deserve a visit. What's more, I discovered the magic of a cruise on the waters of the Moskva in winter. If you had been with me, I am certain that you would agree.

Alas, I must now end this postcard (although my handwriting is small I'm starting to run out of space, seeing as I had lots of things to tell you). What's more, I don't have the means to stay in Moscow for more than two or three days. It's a shame but I am certain that I will love the next city I visit. Next stop, New York! How it is wonderful to travel...

Best wishes,

Your loving Dagmar.

0We could call it Vesta.

What?0

0The book.

?0

Woody… likes to grin out of intellectual satisfaction.

…Woody brings all the notes together.

The country; Mars; The kosmos. Where's the warmth?

Woody was young when he first saw the Gorgon, who was another one of the Villains from an earlier tome, *The Zeroes*, renamed.

"Wordsearch":

Beats of doom. Violent rush. Metronomic seven. While Woody (>Dagmar) still has ears. No obscenity. Whips and centripetal forces. The launchpad is built at last! The earthy state persisted. Let the equations ignite, or at least get hot a bit. Woody's aware of coarseness. The choughs are flying about and Dagmar doesn't feel embarrassed. A gravelly wisdom to all this. Made by muddy habits. On and on and it is pleasing to the people of Heortfordshire. It's hard to know how to process these minerals. Purple, or a shade of that. Anguish is universal. Both Woody and Dagmar have had aftershocks of guilt. Cried for days. Evil tempests. Lighthouses swell. Crimson glories. Crimson isn't a character in this letter. Scope for hidings. Words are slippery spin doctors. The arcing planets do their own thing. Do you remember, my silver? I mine with big swings. Gotta make the crafts, and to make the crafts we gotta extract the ores first. Never really understood geography or geology until now. We love with similar cadences. Venus to the north, Mars to the west. All my love. Woody's deltoids ache. He's been mining all night. The yellow earth only gives up its secrets after a hell of a fight.

Pink strength – Woody. No complete, endless families; no torcs of families. Just us. I remember the darkness of that day and the brightness around the crown. Knee aches a bit. Sickly. Lonely scholar life. I am a silver, leonine god. You are not a silver, leonine god. That's you. What is KERN? Favourite thing in life? Those long pipes in the earth. How is your surrealist teaching going? Would you like a frozen slice of stargazy pie, sweetheart? Gish gallop of a letter. I am unimpressed. Naff music here. My brain is a pearl I shall not place before swine. Woody is a man happy with crass reductionisms. His voice chimes, but too simply and sweepingly. Sorry about all the adverbs, Woody says apologetically.

22:03, 2 December ¬

Dear Professor,

What has gone wrong? I hear you have withdrawn into a rigid routine of solvable second order differential equations. This will not protect you from the inevitable losses. What about our bismuth quest? What about that, huh? Huh?

Call me when you get this.

Yours in conniption,

DAGMAR JACARANDA*

P.S. *I'm trying this cognomen on for size. Let me know what you think!

Midday, 12/01

Hey Dagmar,

I find your name game is top-tier, very sassmeisterly. Many nights of great memeing await you, or did await you or will await you – my grasp on old Father Time is getting pretty shaky. As for the des, they're getting on just fine with me. Got to paddle sometimes. Someone's at the gate someone's got within the gates. A fellow bismuth seeker, perhaps? I shall go down forthwith.

Take care, Dagmar.

PROFESSOR WOODY REDWOOD

There's often phlegm in my throat…

I came to find you, Dagmar cut in. And indeed she had, and had found Woody chilling in a secluded part of his Gothic ancestral mansion of mathematical ideas. Bismuth is what we're in this novel to find, not answers to things we already know, not inner peace. A greyish-white metal used in alloys or in compounded form in medicines: bismuth. Bi. Proton number eighty-three. Likes French cinema. Hates tennis unless a British player's winning.

What about the Wedding? asked Woody.

"We will get around to that," Dagmar stated.

You have speech marks, Woody pointed out.

"Yes," came the reply.

Woody got on with enough things to fill his head. He's getting through it and he'll eventually get that gift. Stuff's got to be passed through, that's his philosophy at present. Not all the things to come are bad. In the grand scheme of things… the grand scheme of things… love marriages…Woody sets a falsifiable example. …Fell memories… the past… Story breaking apart again… Woody doesn't want to forget. He loves it too much. It's Southern Ingland; I, the narrator, am including Kornwall in SI. Just call it Britain, stop mucking about. Conflict, but Woody's toughing things out. Now, the stars. Space travel. Calculus. Geometric distributions; areological distributions. Woody loves mathematics, though he doesn't understand a great deal of it. He eats maths the way men eat food.

Anyway, his missus, Dagmar, has been kidnapped. So the man's got to wheezily make his way across a large swath of Ingland (or England) in order to save her from the bad guy's clutches. And save Britain! You were expecting King Arthur, were you not? ******* Woody is trying to pull himself up to the rank of gentleman. No need for any mathematical analogies here. Who can really be bothered with probability density functions? Woody, some days.

Lots of lilac and remarkable things happen. The quest, a quest! Dagmar was once on trial for saying mean things about her species. Sa iraa. The lady is now a de-escalator, and so is Woody. Neither have broken up their integrity, though. :) Giant telescopes grow out of the English countryside. Two charges, Devon and Cornwall, are separated by only a diameter. The Diameter of Devon, that dismissed, janner-filled county. Are we talking about electrics again? White on green, underrated.

Consumption of paper and differentiation is not its own reward; alphas and ninas (powers of n) samba instead. Vocabularies of dance are the feckless Woody's lullabies. A misplaced minus sign could bring the whole dance system crashing down, so be careful. Avoid the algebra of repulsion, Woody counsels Dagmar (this sounds like *Jabberwocky*); Dagmar says nowt as she examines the unusual bath products the hotel in Old Welwyn has provided. The bad guy, whoever he is, is dully ominous. Of course, the bad guy might be Dagmar's possibly zombified twinless twin Malmesbury!

Woody understands little of Dagmar's character, at least in this book. Can we say she's a blonde? She's a blonde. A gingery blonde. Could be wrong. Will probably be contradicted. Just trying to entertain here.

WOODY

Shush, Narrator. (puts his finger on his lips).

Woody spoke a bit of silence and the story continued. To be a gentleman, yes, and to find his wife, who is in a bit of peril but nothing too bad. Woody's not stunned by stuff. He just writes, writes on, writes equations in his neat handwriting, remembers Navier-Stokes and Black-Scholes. The information equation (if not a then b) arabesques a bit. Woody has mixed feelings about derivatives. When he goes to the barber's he asks for curly dees. Woody's fit bod is tattooed with equations. Anyway, one of his current challenges, in the uncanny country in which he lives, is to tidy the cardboard boxes that he made himself. Insert your own interpretation at your leisure! Leisure. Such a pleasant word; it's a shame Yanks can't say it properly. Never mind. As long as people know what you mean. Ns > es.

WOODY [with half a mind on an insect bite]

The boxes!

NARRATOR (doing something similar to an exorcism)

Sorry, sir, I'm coming to them. U r the pilot, after all. (Woody begins work furiously and assiduously).

WOODY

(grumbles) Changing my plans. Who does this artificer think he is?

ORFEUS

I'm an egalitarian. I want to live in peace with everybody.

DAGMAR

Our modern country…

WOODY [plugging in the orotund vacuum cleaner]

Our country, MML. Wot a mess! We need the American ideal of egalitarianism, not this NP-esque mélange of accent, race and class. (lights a match on a square of sandpaper on his mahogany desk).

DAGMAR

Cr*key M*ses, you've hit the nail on the tetuh.

WOODY

Those landings last spring... The First Consul's face pink... my first thought was that Romanian dictator.

DAGMAR

Now my granny's getting frozen. One hundred and fifty-three, she is.

WOODY [with the sadness of King Lear]

Rotters. I was cryogenically frozen once, in a previous book.

DAGMAR

You've always been a cold fish.

WOODY

Yep.

DAGMAR [downcast]

I didn't mean that. I'm sorry.

WOODY [remembering a chick flick and a choral recital]

Rising causes resentment?

DAGMAR

Probably. (lights a cigarette) Anyway, I love. I'm banally heroic and banally evil.

WOODY

I've had a myriad of stolid mornings since March MMXXX.

DAGMAR

Has your giddy potential gone to waste?

WOODY

IDK. There is that of G*d within everyone.

DAGMAR

I'm a Catholic.

WOODY

So am I.

DAGMAR [loading ORFEUS' dishwasher]

I've joined a side, but I might not stay committed when the sewage comes in.

WOODY

You mean, when the floods return.

DAGMAR

Yeah. When H_2O wants its pounds of flesh.

WOODY

I've really scratched my life.

DAGMAR [buying tissues]

How?

WOODY

I wanted gentle artistic escapes. Beautiful painting and let's plays. But my trunk has become chunky, my arms as skinny as pipe cleaners. I'm a walker, not a cyclist.

DAGMAR [beholding a book]

You're saying lots of things. The joins between your sentences are not visible to me.

WOODY [luckily]

I beg you listen, if you can.

DAGMAR

I am trying. [looks stage right = R]

WOODY

It's hard to sniff out themes. Even at their best, stories centred around themes can feel like overlong public information films.

DAGMAR [thinking deeply]

Themes. Have you ever been on a roller coaster?

WOODY

Nope, just the Big Dipper in Knightsfield.

DAGMAR

Elegant, small. The west side of Welwyn Garden City.

WOODY [yawning]

And now I'm old, really old.

DAGMAR

And you're seeking, what, exactly?

WOODY [with a chord progression]

Bismuth!

DAGMAR [washing behind her ears]

And your maths?

WOODY [doing press-ups during the adverts]

Maths? Maths is great, but I was a coward with it. I'm wary of sitting on my batty for too long.

DAGMAR [opening a textbook from the 1960s]

Most people live constricted lives.

WOODY [slowly, with great gravity]

Nonsense! People find the time for leisure pursuits, loved things ooze out of the constraints.

DAGMAR

Do you remember linear programming? [takes a long drag]

WOODY

How could I forget? [exhales] The Thirties weren't all bad, but I was a bad basketter. Too young to be discerning, too afraid to ask for help. [pause of 2.2] There was a cheerful defeatism at times.

DAGMAR

You got stuck in several pools of mud.

WOODY

Yep. Someone could make a short black comedy out of it. When I was wandering around Ziggurat Yoon hearing commands in my head I didn't act on. Considering getting a carbine and a dangerous whisk.

DAGMAR [however the actress wishes to interpret]

That must have been awful.

WOODY [revising compositions]

Maybe the commands were God's warnings. Like my sneezes and aches.

DAGMAR [renting a caravan in the commentariat]

You ache a lot, don't you? [stubs out the ciggie, which magically disappears].

WOODY [thinking of entertainment]

You get used to it, which is terrible, 'cos the aches worsen like wars.

DAGMAR [clicks]

The giddiness needs a whale. Your stomach. That's the base. The base for all the hijinks, all the talking dogs and scratches.

WOODY [preparing to be interviewed by Roman Cleeve]

Yep. [unzips his backpack and takes out a cider].

DAGMAR [tidying]

I rant too much. I emit low groans.

WOODY

This is a proper convo. I am fatigued.

DAGMAR [mistily]

Absolumente.

WOODY [opening the Carolean fridge]

Want a cyder?

DAGMAR

Yeah mate.

WOODY

[takes a can out and gives it to her, then slumps onto the tasty settee]

I remember all the Jovian stuff in the Forties. I'm every man's bro, but no one should think of me as their bro.

DAGMAR

[drinks gustily from her can]

My bathroom's a pain to clean. I'm working class; I won't get servants.

WOODY

Good exercise innit though? [shows off his biceps]

DAGMAR

Get you, Mr Universe.

WOODY

Anyway, how's your career, beautiful lady from Southern Asian Somewhere?

DAGMAR

I'm not Southern Asian. Really, I'm just a Wiccan scout.

WOODY [mystified]

Wiccan? Wicca? What in the future is that?

DAGMAR

Summat hellbound. Whatevs. I'm pretty Catholic. But power should not always come from the centre. [finishes can and raids Woody's backpack].

WOODY

[pretending not to notice]

It's all so odd and guarded, isn't it? Like we're all prim robots, or summat.

DAGMAR

East side of Welwyn Garden City. It's all flats now.

WOODY [slowly, with great gravity]

It was flat when I was there.

DAGMAR

Where do you live nao?

WOODY [briefly observing fine dust]

Trade secret.

DAGMAR

Fair do's. [opens her new can]

WOODY

[pats his belly] Gotta get going now. Fighting against frustration and yucky stoof.

DAGMAR

Righty. What your name, hunkybun? [opens her can]

WOODY

Redwood. Professor Woody Redwood.

DAGMAR [plugging in a handheld video game console to charge]

Mind 'ow ya go, Redwood. Don't keel over 2nite, it'll be real bad for ya.

WOODY

Will do – won't do. See ya hoodlum-Persephone chick.

DAGMAR

[raises palm in farewell]

[WOODY opens a trapdoor in the stage and goes down through it]

DAGMAR

[to herself]

All on me own. Not for the first time. Wanting… wanting to feel less. Stultify myself, give the inside of my skull pins and needles. The underclass am I. Nah. I don't believe in classes. I'm egalitarian. I'm a libertarian as well. I've tattoos of Ayn Rand on my knees and elbows. I am a fiend of the present age. The establishment tried long ago to control me, to empty me of sap. I rebelled, rebelled. [quickly] Very quietly, I rebelled. I am Brittish. [takes a big swig].

[Lights gaslamps flicker three times]

DAGMAR [with breeziness]

Must be the rise in energy bills.

[The lights go out a final time]

End of Act 2 of 3

Act 3

WOODY

[a voice resounding in the blue darkness]

Nature is not forgiving to us when we do things on impulse. Hello, audience. [the lights go on, a faint blue haze remains over the stage].

WOODY

Where is Act 1? Later. Look back in the book. Page 5? 6? Come on, Narrator, give me summat.

DAGMAR

[climbing out of the stage trapdoor]

Another night in the cells. Like a beehive. I've often got beehives in my bonnet. 120 degree internal angle. Hi Woody.

WOODY

Sup, lady.

DAGMAR [leading in a whippet, Val (it's him!)]

Oh, what a fine day.

WOODY

No time for self care these days. Modern Briten is harsh and humourless. I've had to become an 'ard b*stard in order to get to the day centre and back. I've given up plonk as well. No more cyder for me.

DAGMAR

You're not squiffy?

WOODY

Nah.

DAGMAR

That's good. No money in social care, is there?

WOODY

Nope.

DAGMAR

"Women's work." That's what they told me at the castle.

WOODY

Can't argue with that.

DAGMAR

I get migraines.

WOODY

I tried to find you. I tried to find you.

DAGMAR [with a square root]

What?

WOODY

When you were 'napped. I quested you and I got you back, my love.

DAGMAR

I've stopped the footie.

WOODY [convulsing a little]

Oh yeah?

DAGMAR

Yeah, it served its time. Five year periods, you know. Gotta professionalise meself.

WOODY

Good lass. Be careful with what you do.

DAGMAR

Cheers. I've chucked the booze in too.

WOODY

Best thing for it. Thaler sink.

DAGMAR

It's all beautiful, hard-won recoveries, isn't it?

WOODY [opens the back door to put the recycling out]

Yep. Undoubtedly.

DAGMAR

Getting some space in my head. Not rushing to fill da shelves.

WOODY

Y'all right. [in an Appalachian drawl] Nickles and dimes. Pounds and pennies. Boycers!

DAGMAR [measuring a pool of lava]

Garden Briten. Not Great Briten.

WOODY

Tempters here. The aftershocks go on for aeons.

DAGMAR

Professor?

WOODY [sorting the recycling into n piles to go in the $n+1$ bags]

Yes, hoodlum?

DAGMAR [visiting a haunted house in another reality]

Do you think we're archetypal characters?

WOODY

[snorts] Of course we are not, my lady.

DAGMAR

You're clever. You're quick.

WOODY

Faster than a dart, Dagmar.

DAGMAR

My 'ero.

WOODY

Yo, girlie. We can be chums, yes, but nowt more than that.

DAGMAR

Oh, ok.

WOODY [reddening]

Y'all right Dagmar?

DAGMAR

Sure, yep, sure. I'm not gonna stalk you or moonlight as your murderer or something.

WOODY [eating sugar cubes as if they were hallucinogenic berries]

Good 2 no.

DAGMAR

Are you proud of moi?

WOODY

'Course. You've been through the collapses, macheted through the c-r-*-p. You're witty and helpful, if a bit somnolent. You're the best.

DAGMAR

[smiles lopsidedly] Good 2 no.

WOODY

Innit.

DAGMAR

You're a good fella too. You don't put extraneous info in your telegrams.

WOODY

Nope, not at all. Coupla dots & dashes & then I'm out of yr electric hair.

DAGMAR [pondering quality]

My friends say the same.

WOODY

Your togs are pretty nice. English chic. 2007 for ever.

DAGMAR [with fondness]

I had a lot of liquid lunches back then.

WOODY

I was desperate for my papers to be read.

DAGMAR

What's your field?

WOODY

Electromagnetic.

DAGMAR

Shocking.

WOODY [with a smirk like a wiggly millipede]

And attractive.

DAGMAR

Rake.

WOODY [attention caught by a bountiful olive tree]

I beg your pardon? What the 'ell are you sayin'?

DAGMAR

Rake. Rake I said. Take a chill pill with water.

WOODY

Sorry. Sorry. *Mi dispiace.*

DAGMAR

My jaw's tiring from all this talking.

WOODY [thinking about using his kiln]

Mine too, though... not so much, I think.

DAGMAR [after stretching her jaw with a bookmark]

I'll be silent. Once, I went horribly barmy.

WOODY

OK.

Woody is a dabbler, a jack of all trades. Just trying to help, impersonally, like a benevolent spirit. A protagonist in a platforming game. Remember Abbott's novel?

WOODY

You spelled his name right this time! [thumbs up]

LIGHTS OUT

End of Act 3. *Thunderbolt* columnists, do your write-up now, plz.

A JAZZ SOLO, reader's discretion.

And waters rose over Southern England. Deucalion's deluge. The water's rather, erm, brackish! ...new filtration tech is online... otters are knitting waterproof socks.

Woody says his messy life is a lifetime's work. The author could say something about an eternal summer here, but will not.

WOODY [to the heavens]

I'm still a gamer above everything else. That's my punt at immortality.

DAGMAR

[proudly] He's not a snob.

WOODY

She's an autodidact.

DAGMAR

I don't chase drama; that's a race to the bottom. Humorous mythological content, *that's* my forte.

[A plastic tree falls with a mild thunk onto the stage].

WOODY

[sagely] Nature cannot bear too high taxes.

DAGMAR [fancifully]

I like bears.

WOODY

Me too! I like koalas.

DAGMAR

KoalaSleep, is that your moniker?

WOODY [with a merry grin]

It will be, next time I boot up a heliograph.

DAGMAR

Messages only by daylight. Snazzy.

WOODY [nodding]

Innit.

DAGMAR

Have you ever heard the story of the Antikythera Mechanism?

WOODY

The primitive computer?

DAGMAR

Yes.

WOODY [smiling]

I have.

[There is a sudden earthquake and Woody and Dagmar fall to the floor].

WOODY [in rising pitch]

Ow. Ow. Ouch.

DAGMAR

Woody!

WOODY [getting rather chilly]

I'm here. In pain.

DAGMAR

Would you like me to give you the Last Rites?

WOODY [panting]

Jumping the gun! I'll be all right. I survived the Martian war.

DAGMAR [relieved]

Righto. I've another book to get to. Will you be all right on your own?

WOODY [laughs fondly]

'Course I won't. Love ya.

DAGMAR

Shall I stop off at the offie on my way back?

WOODY [seeming wise and ancient]

Not this time. I am resisting addiction. There be many addictions about these days

DAGMAR [at the exit]

Ta-ra Woody.

WOODY

Ta-ra.

[he sighs heavily and takes a blackcovered Bible out of his backpack. He stares at the front cover]

Holy Bible.

[after 2 seconds the lights go down].

Woody is in Hell. His feet have been replaced with chattering skulls. Very hard to walk on. Saten, who might be Satan (in Cornish he's called 'Satnas'), always starts with the important areas.

SATEN

[smiles] I can see your wings. How long do you think you'll stay?

WOODY [staring aghast at his transformed feet]

As long as the narrator allows.

SATEN

I was going to expound on *Paradise* Lost, but I'll let you get on.

WOODY

See ya.

[Saten vanishes in a puff of smoke. Woody exhales].

WOODY

Not exactly Miltonic, was he? I suppose writing for the *Thunderbolt* chipwrapper makes you less articulate. Anyway [moves onto his hands and knees] Let's explore this aphysical place. [he goes through a narrow, green corridor and his strong and functional black maple-leaflike wings get a bit squished].

WOODY [scanning the *Thunderbolt* headlines on 08/06/2050]

You know, ORFEUS, I don't have a clue what is going on.

ORFEUS HOPP

[booming voice] Think Orpheus, Woody.

WOODY

Hmm? I can't play a single note, though. Too dyspraxic.

ORFEUS

Have a look at this! [drops a book into Woody's realm]

WOODY

[picks up the book and reads the title]

The Land of Recovered Comfort

ORFEUS [unashamed]

Oh. That's not a playing textbook.

WOODY [running his left hand through his attractive long hair]

Well, I can flick some frets and I can touch some piano keys.

ORFEUS [calling up a speedrun of *Summer In Sapporo V* on his computer]

Let's see if we can go back…

   Father, who roused me with promises of gudgeon-fishing, hiking and Horace, I thank you. This book exists airily, and I want it to be airier still, even though there's only a small chance of that happening. Air, Earth, Fire, Water. I'm over-nervous and melodramatic, or I was. The teeth of time press on me. One more book of *The Odyssey*…

ORFEUS [finger on chin]

Have you ever played *Summer in Sapporo VI*?

WOODY [blowing his nose. Hayfever!]

No. Have you?

ORFEUS

No. But I have read of it.

SATEN [re-entering through a stage door with great masochism]

With whom do you speak, Woody?

[a ferocious and well-whetted javelin, thrown by ORFEUS, flies down from the eaves and kills Saten].

ORFEUS [alert, eyes shining]

Flee, Woody, flee! Climb up the ladder!

WOODY

[climbs breathlessly]

ORFEUS [barking]

Pace yourself, sonny jim! It's a very long ladder.

WOODY

Isn't it always?

End of scene 4.

WOODY

[still climbing]

I know it's not good to talk about religion in books, but it's what interests the writer.

ORFEUS [grumpily]

Gotta use the tools at hand.

WOODY

I'm a frustrated middle class aspirant.

ORFEUS [finger on chin]

What does that have to do with religion? [to Dagmar going down her own ladder] Hi, Dag.

WOODY

[horrifically concerned] What's going to happen to her?

ORFEUS [as compassionately as a mother to her chicks]

Nothing dreadful.

WOODY [assuaged, then, with adoration:]

See you in Magaluf, Dagmar.

DAGMAR

[nods, keeps descending]

ORFEUS [eating]

A takeaway. From the Great Red Dragon restaurant. [to Woody] Time constraints are brutal, aren't they?

WOODY [pausing to speak clearly]

Yeah. Choose your whale, I say. Sunshine falls after the rain, but what if you got lost in the rain? What if you got so befuddled you forgot about the sunshine? What if your goals were too vague and weak to make the rain meaningful?

ORFEUS [understanding what Woody is on about]

One clear day, maybe twelve in a year, might be all you get.

WOODY

Yes. I'm feeling like Job.

ORFEUS

Keeping yourself safe. Scabbard the sharp edges.

WOODY

Doing so.

ORFEUS

Those walks in 2044-45.

(2.3)

WOODY

My golden years.

ORFEUS [sighs]

You need to recover that motor.

WOODY

You mean, that tractor?

ORFEUS

Yes.

WOODY [surprised]

The one I threw in the old pond?

ORFEUS

Yep.

WOODY

Outdoor leisure saved me. The sylvan jobs.

ORFEUS

Many things have saved you, not least yourself.

WOODY [with one last look at his self-pity]

I needed a lot of saving.

ORFEUS

(with strange emphases) Like an unreliable computer.

WOODY

There are few hardy novelists like me today (c.2050).

ORFEUS [wearily]

The middle class are turning into the underclass, like moths.

WOODY [like a bear]

Theme for a novel, that.

ORFEUS

When do you think we'll turn back in2 prose?

WOODY

Soon enuf.

[silence]

ORFEUS

I can't stand certain circles. Too many fell and smooshing haunters of religion and politics.

WOODY

When I knew of such misers, I just thought, "that's the way of the world." Demons stalk the earth.

 [A bit of mizzle falls].

ORFEUS [exclaims]

Aqua! Aqua!

WOODY

Why are you always repeating yourself?

ORFEUS

Because I'm your hapless brain. [smiles evilly]

WOODY [with great weariness; evil is in everyone]

Shut it, mate [pauses on the metaphysical ladder]

ORFEUS

How are you really, pilgrim soul?

WOODY

At this mo, in need of assistance. Gimme some strength, please.

ORFEUS [with competitiveness]

What's your relationship with Xianity?

WOODY [rapidly]

I hide behind its coattails – and the Roman Church is the biggest religion around – for protection. I love the reds and golds of the Roman Church. But I don't fancy being a martyr. There is so much evil and short-termism around us. I struggle to believe anyone could do anything for the public good.

ORFEUS

You know that beliefs are not always falsifiable?

WOODY

Depends how you believe them. Inside, in the churn of you… [scratches scalp with both hands, which is a hard thing to do when you're on a ladder].

ORFEUS [trying to find what Woody cherishes]

Tell me about your mathematics.

WOODY [more attentive now]

Do you mean, what mathematics means to me?

ORFEUS

Yes.

WOODY

[mildly puzzled] Why not say that? It was a humorous maze, an anaesthetic, a backdrop and an analgesic. All of those at once. You know how it is in the country these days: people fall through the cracks. That's all I have to say.

[A C# note is struck for two seconds]

ORFEUS

[not unkindly]

What do you want, Woody?

WOODY

Some speech marks. And better health. And possibly some bismuth.

Orfeus waved his oaken wand and speech marks appeared in the corner of Woody's mouth.

ORFEUS

Woody, I give you the gift of free speech.

"Thank you, sir," said Woody, his mind half on pancakes. "I'll be sure to acknowledge you later on. Thank you. Thank you."

And like a cresting dolphin Woody returned to the surface of the river, his dated duds stuck to him…

19th July 2050

To the new Mister and Mistress Halberd,

Congratulations to you two lovebirds, Chix and Edgar, on your amazing romantic journey!! We have been in your corner since day one!! We love you and wish you all the best with everything you do!!

Yours sincerely,

Woody & Dagmar

I need you, Dagmar Jacaranda, realised Professor Woody Redwood. I need you and I need the bismuth. Not to make profit, nor to exorcise a personal ghost, nor still to roll about in nostalgia. Bismuth's a beauty I'd like to observe. But Dagmar could not hear him. And so Woody trudged on through Tetra on the summer day on which this story takes place, a double quest in his mind, to find the metal and his girl.

"Bother," said Dagmar, after she had awoken in Halberd's castle. A spooky Gothic door creaked open. A lumpen fiend, the wealthy and misshapen Tyran Halberd walked in through the gap. His fingernails were unusually long, Dagmar noted.

Boredom. Boredom. Boredom. Boredom like a fog. Like a deathly fog. That is what Dagmar felt when she woke up. Boredom. Languid, fearful boredom. She felt oafish, so oafish. Unglamorous. Wound up. In an emotionally cold room in a chamber belonging to a rich man. Very functional architecture. Tyran, her gaoler, was off somewhere, counting his ores. Hence, Dagmar used her brief solitude wisely.

Tyran entered the room jollily. He'd left the door open, you see. Tyran's a benevolent fellow, in the vein of Timon of Athens and Messieurs Xavier Vector and Jarrett Palmer (that printing geek with a heart of gold). Tyran exudes generosity and warmth. No need to hear him speak. This scene, this volume, of Dagmar and Tyran won't be some fruitless screwball scene. No shot-reverse-shot. Oh no. Warmth above the mine. Copper and tin and arsenic and possibly bismuth are getting dug out of Terra as we speak. It's 1849 now. The narrator can change time just like that.

Ahem, coughed Tyran, to Dagmar. You will notice that you are separated from that Redwood oaf, that fiend of general grumbles.

Dagmar's dudgeon went high at this insult:

"You don't know the first thing about him, Tyran, smarmy worm of the mining world. He's a man of honour. His brain has been damaged by life's pollution – your pollution – the pollution from your industry!"

Tyran raised his chin as the lady went on. "Madam," he said, with all the unctuousness of a do-gooder, "if it was not for my *industry*, as you call it, and the Croesusian wealth that is brings, there would be no social progress of any kind. You would be a toothless beggar in the circular city before you were out of your swaddling. I bid you be silent."

"It's not all about being," Dagmar protested. "I do not wish a slab on my chest forever. We live in a brutal age. Your energetic indifference to the plight of men is a sad thing. One sad thing, maybe, Woody's unsteady health, but I'm an individualist, not a statistician. One atom."

The thrust of Dagmar's speech was beyond Tyran. Writing essays on the same theme would probably prove fruitless as well. Tyran popped out of the room and Dagmar returned to her inner reflections. Woody! Woody! Where was that poor scamp? And, with a tip of her hat to the upcoming wedding, Dagmar also pondered the location of the bismuth. Had it really been discovered in Tyran's mineworks? Could it be dragged out? What superstitions surrounded this benevolent metal incongruously habitant in the poisoner's corridor? Dagmar resolved to solve these things. She was also excited about *Summer in Sapporo VIII*.

Her training – from novels – entered her head. Try to escape as quickly as you can! Dagmar tried the windows – invisibly barred. Likely to give you a nasty static shock. A priest-hole behind the bookcase? There was always one in the novels Dagmar liked to read. Not in this particular real situation. Dagmar took a gander under the bed, which was eerily dust-free. Nope. No tools for mêlée. Not even a fishing rod or a *Thunderbolt* editorial. Anger Tyran when he gets back?

Dagmar's not good at explaining problems. She can't narrate her own actions, except when she's doing audio description. She hates to plan things out from scratch. She walked to the door Tyran through which had entered, turned the tungsten knob – unlocked! – and passed through. Security!

Sinister music here. Get out your violins and theremin. This is lighter fare than the other ones. Hopefully this lightness will stay a trend. How much can you really narrate? The burger queue moves if you're wanting…

Dagmar briefly thought about Edgar, that moody dude with his perfunctory experiments. A dude with a busier head than he knew what to do with. Dagmar thought about her own experiments in her writing career (commenced 1842). Writing is easy, Dagmar would tell her friends at the balls. Forming a good writing habit, now that I find difficult.

Dagmar's a bit of a blowsy woman, a bit loud, a bit camp, but she's a blonde bear of a female. The narrator's got a soft spot for her. As an aside, the narrator has grown tired of experiments. Finally at the nineteenth century peak, the great entertainments! 'Course, you could make a case for *Tom Jones* and *Tristram Shandy* as entertainments. Dagmar likes *Pamela*. She angers quickly, like Tom Jones.

Art, art, that thing. You can't be entertained by what bowls you over, thinks Dagmar. A very sensitive lady. She's still in Tyran's castle, by the way. This young lady, the heroine of our tale, doesn't open her heart easily. That red organ does flutter, a bit, with the promise of love. The writing of this, the writing of this! Time on one's batties at the typewriter well spent!

Technology comes first, Dagmar reminded herself… if you don't rush it, nothing happens. Technology spread its vague tentacles far and wide, to be coloured in later. Thanks, petal.

Tyran is a man of brittle petals, brittle layers, brittle icy rings far from a shallow, hot-tempered centre. Some unknown force or forces keep him from collapsing like a shattered mining tool.

So difficult! So much weariness! But just putting ores into the computer. There we go.

Dagmar wants to marry Woody. Does he want to marry her? Miss Jakespeare can hunt down her enemies if she wants, end their bloodlines and their friends. The state and judiciary have condemned them; no authority can stop her. She still wants to marry Woody, though, and do right by him. Most of the world's horrors issue not from malice but from decay and a marriage might arrest unhappy rotting.

Tyran re-entered the room bearing an incongruous sandwich. Dagmar had gone like those New England colonists.

So many stops and starts are unavoidable! This modern world, of 1849, without signposts! Still got plenty of stagecoaches, though.

Dagmar's in Tyran's voluminous library. Aquamarine curved spines jut out at her; these are Dagmar's beloved cylinders. So gorgeous! So many tales! Hoffmann, Grimm, von Kleist…

Dagmar sleeps and fights hard. She is that kind of lady, a she-wolf of a woman, believes Tyran. Jakespeare is probably not her surname. Maybe it's Japes. It's hard to survive castles. Our young lady opens the bronze boards and begins to read the black text on the thin brown pages.

Dagmar doesn't duck confrontation. But she's also a reader *ab utero*. Tyran, kindly jailer, also possesses many medical tomes.

Blood, phlegm, yellow bile, black bile, all the fabulous humours. Bodies are not as well ordered as Dagmar had once thought. Her imagination went to a gold lab in the warm future, one of great machines and mysterious vials.

The train of Dagmar's eyes go on, never pausing, as she reads and reads. A pleasant pile in the tradition of Nennius mounts up. Read books; a heap. But a good heap. Re-reads are for the hereafter, Dagmar tells Tyran, perhaps in error. Good day, sir.

How many messes, how many rushes, are obscured by print and boards! <= Dagmar had yet to think that statement.

At night the lullaby of the mines went on and on.

Dagmar continued with her accomplishments. Reading for pleasure. Does she need a husband?

The mines beneath; Tyran, a score of years prior, had resolved to make a success of himself. Had he? The machines' groans laudanummed his soul. Never a perfect seam though, is there, to pose an impertinent question. The soul's pretty hard to grasp, is it not, tycoon? Dictators want perpetual skittishness.

I hope your readings are going well, stated Tyran one bleary morning. The weather's changing again, isn't it? Tlaloc's odd in these parts, isn't he?

Dagmar held her tongue. She did not digress. She battled fiends in her exquisite mind. She was presently more interested in the physical realm than the mental.

"Zombies don't need couches," spoke the young lady.

A feverish, unshaven doubt shook Tyran's rigid heart. His young captive had clearly acquired inky goggles. He left a snack in the dumb waiter and then he left.

An hour is a long time. Dagmar's new book is already old. So many grandiose empathy machines. Dog-eared big hearts. Morning is one day; afternoon another.

Dagmar, action heroine, is able to get into the minds and bodies of others. What a lass! "An amazon!" exclaims Tyran. "A strong combatant, stern and wise, yet, like all women, she knows how to sit on a lilypad and relax. Stern!"

Mining. Tyran knows that industry well. He's an iron-strong gentleman. He has no need for dread drivers; his miners are happy to work for him.

There are endless articles from worrywarts to be found in the local *Thunderbolt* newspaper. Dagmar doesn't read "chipwrappers". No interest, not even a negative interest. They are the detritus of the future, in her estimation.

Tyran treads gently on the soft carpets in his castles. He lives, it will hopefully be clear, neither sarcastically nor sycophantically and he's happy that Dagmar's reading seems to be going excellently. The castle's unsmug and incorrupt.

An elf wandered into the book, realised she was in the wrong tome, and walked out again, crumpling her cheeks in apology and turning down her head. No need to fret, dear, comforted Dagmar.

Tyran ordered more books for Miss Jakespeare. "Novels, like all books, have state," stated the lady when she received them. Tyran switched off. All was unpleasant cyclones outside, but Dagmar stayed with her companions of wood fibre. *The Posthumous Papers of the Pickwick Club* tickled her heart. Tyran stuck to reading the hastily written reports delivered to him about the conditions in his own mines. Ledgers were not his affairs. Accounts were Woody's business, but he was missing, so Tyran ignored them.

A chough flew over the castle-mine complex. "That is certainly a chough," said Tyran, as the *pyrrhocorax pyrrhocorax* soared above.

One day, at six in the morning, Dagmar asked Tyran about feldspar, but Tyran knew nothing about that mineral.

To-day. Dagmar thought a bit. "People wish to conserve for a reason," she said aloud.

Tyran muttered something unpleasant about Woody. Casual cruelty, p'raps?

"What did you say about my sweetheart," Dagmar snarled to Tyran, her robust heart set to flame like a ruby under charcoal. "For all his faults, for all his many faults, that man has been a noble friend of mine through my life. He has helped me without ceasing. Last night I dreamt of floating metal platforms with flint edges. Woody is mine, and I have not forgotten him. Don't forget yourself, *sir*."

Tyran mumbled something apologetic and quitted the room, his posture become that of a humiliated servant. He felt hot, quite hot, like a pool of water into which an alkali metal has just been dropped. Embarrassed, he sucked great gollops of air into his lungs. Meanwhile, his calm captive resumed her reading, persisting perhaps just a bit too long in her perusal of an alchemical tome she already knew backwards.

DATE: 3rd December 2050

HALBERD MINES

My darling Woody,

Like the loyal Penelope I await your return most ardently. Another year has passed. I hope your exertions have not over-wearied you. Have you read the works of Henry Fielding?

With a kind heart and strong frame,

Dagmar Jakespeare

Guilt – as opposed to shame – was rare to trouble the severe personage of Mr Tyran Halberd, but heavy roast dinners – which he consumed alone at one end of a dark quartz table – increasingly hurt his corporeal form. His increasing girth gave him pains in his guts as he breathed and moved. *Just engage in some energetic movements,* Mr Halberd read the notes his physician, Doctor Fell, had written for him and placed on his desk, *and eat less meat.*

Tyran henceforth increased his ambling around his rooms while his mineworkers toiled laboriously below. What a court of alien dreams were those unseen pits! Dens of sturdy men and elves and sliding devices! The earth goddess granted great amounts of tin, copper and bismuth to the men, but not before terrible struggles. Dagmar grimaced in her soul when she learned the perilous truth… There are violent sins in this world, sins greater than smiling during a tango…

TYRAN [sweating]

You've never held a rifle, have you, Miss Jakespeare?

DAGMAR [(placing a novel down on TYRAN's wide onyx desk]

No. No. That's unthinkable. I'm British. I use a knife.

TYRAN [wishing to draw out her supernatural abilities]

You have powers of a most occult kind.

DAGMAR [thinking 'hurrah', but not for the reason the reader might think, if the author might attempt telepathy]

Occult?

TYRAN

Hidden. Like Martian ores.

DAGMAR

Mining is not merely about one attacking the earth with a pickaxe.

TYRAN [curling his lip]

Go. Go.

DAGMAR [to herself]

One cannot merely imitate what others do. [to Tyran] Breathe, sir.

TYRAN [quietly, with sharpness]

Go, milady. Leave this room.

Dagmar left. The mine owner stared at the wall as if he could see through it to the edge of our solar system. Order returned to him at the speed of enzymes.

A sensible order of events went by like mine carts on a rail. Tyran loved sensible orders, although none of them are sophisticated. He says "for all that," a lot. His eyes are always wide open. Memories of the era of the Reform Bill haunt him a bit.

One rainy day, one on which the mines below produced relatively little noise, Dagmar discovered complicated examination papers tucked inside a novel of Smollett's. A mathematical paper! A bewitching glow filled the room. The cosine rule bowed before Dagmar and the trusty product rule curtsied. How delightful! Our sage and omnivorous lady was lost for words.

Tyran's begun taking the psychic laudanum in the evenings. He doesn't think his new mining tool will be refunded. Our mine owner struggles to get out of the medieval past. The search for an accurate modern bard is oft a fruitless one. Out of ignorance and self-insecurity, Tyran often makes more of things than what they are. I pray for him.

Dagmar's a 'satholic'; she doesn't take communion. This young lady took down some devils in 2048. Maybe not THE D*vil.

"I fought in the Fifties," said Woody plainly as he sipped his rum. "Harsh. But I thought I was fighting for the right thing, you know."

Dagmar, his aging confidante, watched him from the other side of the table.

"All this is time long past," continued Woody. "I've been tidying."

"Dodging the hill-bound bloke with the rock?" asked Dagmar.

"Yes. My strength is not what it was; my zest has deserted me." Woody cricked his neck. "Now, I'm just a hardy poet and occasional brougham driver. I make decent money shipping doctors and nurses."

Dagmar sipped at her beverage. Her friend stretched his arms.

"I conducted mining experiments," revealed he.

"Oh?"

"Yea. You wouldn't think me experimental. And I wasn't, not really, in those days in the Fifties." *DRINK*

"You can't conduct a sensible experiment if you don't know what it is you're testing."

"Quite. Quite!"

"And now you're bringing amusement like Xavier Vector and Ricoché."

"Yea, yea. I suppose I am."

"You've stopped insulting yourself?"

"Aye. I have stopped insulting myself. Sometimes I fear appearing in public, lest an unruly dragon comes my way—"

"Fear's ubiquitous. Some dragons are villainous."

"—but I know how to have dignity. The quakes in space of late have shaken me."

"You're not alone in that."

Woody smiled at Dagmar. He offered to buy her another drink and she accepted. Woody's brogues squeaked on the old wooden floor of the public house.

"Two shandies please," said the old professor and the canine barman –Val! –behind the mahogany counter took his money and depressed the taps.

One is guarding for others.

Woody's childhood was pretty miserable. Lots of hanging around with dolls in an old shop. A viscous scenery of sensation all around.

In a biplane over Anglesey, ears and scalp chilled by the air, Woody works some stuff out. Aerial downloads worked out pretty well, all things considered. Ordered some hymnbooks to Dagmar's (presents for Yule). Best get it done early. Dagmar dances – rather awkwardly, not as well as her inspiration Tanya – and Schubert is definitely her favourite. The young Miss D. Jakespeare is a Victorian elfin matchmaker, in case you were wondering (if you weren't, that's quite all right). Also a social reformer. She's supernaturally tireless!

BUCK HOUSE,

17/08/2125

Your Majesty,

How can we ensure that the infants of today become the Pitts of tomorrow? The answer, at every level, is education. Without an academic upbringing, our children cannot flourish. However, it pains me to say that the state of our country's schools simply repulse; they fail our young.

From my ten years' experience in schooling, I know first-hand of the barbarity of these institutions. Savage beatings are doled upon our babes with carefree strokes, all to punish the slightest misstep. Even worse, the tyrannical heads of said institutions are more morally bankrupt than any child could ever be! One governor adorned himself in silken garb before encouraging his charge to live as paupers. Such hypocrisy is as grotesque as it is widespread.

*It is not just fat masters who punish our young: filth, dank walls and dire food also stifle their lights. Revolting accommodations disgust the mind and the senses and rob our children of a willing to learn. There are those who claim such poverty will improve our children in the long run, but of these sceptics I point to the latest findings of John Snow, a British doctor. You will remember, Your Majesty, that Doctor Snow proved a conclusive link between unclean conditions and deadly diseases like cholera and typhus. The latter swept like a plague over one of my schools, and fifty babes were struck from history. I implore Your Majesty to think of the loss to the world of those fifty darlings, let alone those who died at other schools of **perfectly preventable diseases.***

Assuming that our babe survives the perils of childhood, where do our offspring go? There is a definite paucity of jobs for middle-class school leavers, and therefore many children find themselves in terminal destitution and unemployment. I know of a young lady, a brilliant, hardworking student and devoted Christian who has yet no prospects for life after education. There is a frighteningly high possibility of her finding herself in the workhouse, and were this travesty to occur, another candle to the future would be blown out.

Moreover, the vast majority of children learn little or no creditable skills during their school studies. In our schools there is a great emphasis on the teaching of Jesus and the Bible. Take me for no heathen, religious studies are wholesome and good, but this cannot be the only thing taught. Practical skills such as engineering and science are the building blocks for personal success and a grand Empire, which must be maintained. British education must improve. The classics are mega, as well. Let Lucan and Aristophanes out of the box, Your Majesty; the ancients are a punnet of well-picked strawberries.

But what can be done about this adverse state of affairs? Well, firstly you, Your Majesty, could found a school inspection system. This organisation would appoint overseers, who would frequently visit schools and report on the circumstances of each school to Parliament. Where necessary, educators deemed 'unsuitable' would be removed and replaced with those who have a better understanding of children and their delicate needs. There can be no tolerance of bullying and intimidation in getting our children to learn. Similarly, a minimum sum must be spent on children's food and lodgings; this should be enforceable by law. The amount need not be much; just enough to keep our children warm, fed and safe from contagion. Building reforms must be introduced as well, to ensure that our young are reared in environments representative of our great Empire. The inferior, stone-cold barracks of the moment must be pulled down. Lastly, there needs to be an introduction of a mandatory curriculum for children to study. This would have to be followed by every school in the country. This curriculum would contain many subjects, such as art and humanities. Later on, students would sit exams in these subjects, and then progress on to study a selection of them at a higher level. Every child would therefore have a standardised set of qualifications, recognised throughout the country. Said qualifications would be necessary to pursue careers in disciplines such as literature and the sciences.

Your Majesty, as revolutionary as these reforms sound, I feel they are utterly necessary in order to inspire our young to reach eminent heights, and to further the Empire's reputation as the finest breeding ground for intellectual development and industry anywhere in the world.

Yours sincerely,

DAGMAR JAKESPEARE

3 Oct 2047: Woody's in the fire and the air. ☺ Stuff's getting sorted ☺ Popular taste these days is quite subtle, varied and innovative. ☺

6 Oct 2047: Chilly weather. The chilly world, Dagmar says. Woody's highlighting his notes on radon, bismuth, aldehydes and alkanes.

7 Oct 2047: What is Tyran Halberd NOT doing?

9 Oct 2047: How's the bismuth quest going?

11 Oct 2047: How's Dagmar's reading going, does she is she gleaning social insights from her book-mates? Mr Halberd says he can make his own mind bigger by reading and mesmerism. Tommyrot, says Dagmar.

13 October 2047: 'Geological' is Tyran's favourite word. Who's typing?

25 October 2047: Where's Tyran's knighthood? Come on, Queen. 'Bit of lèse-majesté there,' interjects Dagmar.

28 October 2047: Reading can be a slow process, declares Dagmar, and patience is its virtue. She's got her hair done nicely today. And her beauty mirror's rather cracked!

7 November 2047: *TH has shewn himself to be an atrocious man,* writes Dagmar.

11 November 2047: This is a section of Woody's diary. He's intentionally keeping the even pages blank. Part of all his maths stuff.

22 Nov 2047: Been doing sit-ups. We can do this, people.

1 Dec 2047: Woody jumps in the morning, but not onto bandwagons.

2 Dec 2047: Time constraints, Dagmar called to Woody. I 'ate timers, says Woody. But I'm 'ating the wrong things, he goes on. I 'ate the freeze I give myself when I 'ave a job to do. Maybe you don't give yourself enough practice, suggests his friend Dagmar.

8 Dec 2047: Dagmar is sick of having enemies.

30 Jan 2048: The world's all base. All poison. I am in the mathematics, announced Woody whence concepts fit together like chemistry.

31 Jan 2048: Waves as perfect as Hamlet or carbon. Could cry.

20 Mar 2048: Living under a haze. Trying to do the right thing and be chirpily entertaining. Was slightly ignored in her sickly childhood.

22 Mar 2048: Dagmar's Top Secret Diary: Time to release the beast a bit. Got to matchmake/datedoc. My passion.

28 Mar 2048: Reading Cervantes & Montaigne.

4 May 2048: I, Dagmar, am a blowsy lass, I must say. I'm shy and I love people, but I need my own space.

16 May 2048: Woody says I'm a wild woman.

21 May 2048: Bit of a fracas between Woody and Chix for my attention. Often the way. Love them both.

11 Apr 2048: Loved Woody's new top hat!! It's got quadrilaterals on its sloped face!

21 Apr 2048: Strengthening my legs for the quickstep.

7 May 2048: Elfin powers make all this messy. I am an elf. I am not moving the goalposts for myself.

10 May 2048: Woody's got a place for his man things, wherein to manage his volcano.

20 May 2048: I spoke to Woody. I asked him, why do you need someone else to lead you on to God? Then we played golf (goff).

23 May 2048: Ate light biscuits.

2 July 2048: Travelled to my home town.

5 August 2048: More kinesis (exercise).

26 September 2048: That was an excellent essay! exclaimed Dagmar. I've just tipped over my glass of water!

16 November 2048: Not found the bismuth yet!

28 January 2049: I'm not going to insult my foremothers by claiming that males can be females, said Woody, soapboxing. And it's an insult to my forefathers to claim that there are females within our ranks.

5 August 2049: Woody took his dog Val in the carriage with him to visit I, Dagmar.

8 August 2049: Your words woke me from my slumber, said Dagmar, to Woodrow. You are not green, but you are my knight.

20 August 2049: Once, Dagmar would have been rambly and afraid, but nevermore.

22 August 2049: Woody rescued the chameleon he had left on the bus. Phew!

2 September 2049: Dagmar's good at not getting swept up with things. She keeps her moral compass well locked.

4 September 2049: A bit of ridicule is an important thing.

16 Sep 2049: Public life has some thorny dragon's tails in it.

21 September 2049: Within some losses – happiness? And bagels.

2 October 2049: Trapped-tête. Needing water. Will put out the babylons (hanging baskets) to-day.

3 October 2049: In the midst of a happy event Woody wonders what on Terra is going on.

5 October 2049: 'Fearful obligations are not a good thing,' says Woody. 'I don't want to be afraid of that fearful Villain who is gone now, reformed on this earth without dying.'

17 December 2049: Virtual reality... ludodore... gamers making marginalia. Reading backwards and forwards. A sieving motion, maybe.

21 December 2049: Woody bought a batch of Basil Brush drink coasters (for his and Dagmar's mugs of tea and the occasional chai latte).

23 December 2049. Woody and Dagmar, reunited after all the gubbins with the huge mine, danced the Argentine Tango together. Ganchos!

Woody's like an energetic ladybird. Flying about a bit, getting coat-hangers and water and popping bread slices into the toaster. Nice guy.

Exhalation. Dagmar's exhaling because she's found the job and found the sacrifices. Woody looked at his companion over the cups. Something embiggens, milady, said Woody, but I can't think what it is.

"Read the *Thunderbolt*," came the reply.

-All these troubles in Lylas, mused Woody, all these selfish, noisy, dissonant groups. Meanest group wins, it seems.

Woody checks the TV ratings in order to know of present reality. He hates brittle vases, so he tries not to do things that can easily go wrong. His bezzie, Dagmar, has been part of a successful movement –

the Kinetic Movement (KM) – that might fissure now that its main aims have been met. Those with comfy Plutarchs can afford to be obstreperous, to morph into moody gyres that take stuff down to the depths. ø With verbal power comes verbal responsibility. The nosy but nice dragonfly that's an escapee of Summerfield hovers presently. Hullo.

: :

How do we win this fight, asked Woody one morning as he waited for the tea to draw up.

We go around the blockers, replied Dagmar. We issue useful, kind spores. The land needs more kindness. Not everything is a meritocratic race. You need different books at different times in your life.

-There's a lot we don't know about Lylas' problems. My position is absolutely clear and I hope it's not a cowardly one. My heart's in one of the country's many rivers. It's a pleasant stream, the river I'm thinking of.

Dagmar drained her tea down to its lees.

*

Now, I recall those old LP videos. *Summer In Sapporo II – VI.* Finally unlocked the Great Sundial. Yep. Ghostly shadows but not malicious ones.

Beowulf. Chaucer. Shakespeare. Those are the men. -Woody

It's all about art with the French, Dagmar grumbled gaily. There's good and bad with that.

People need kindness in this bewildering world, said Woody. However, I do not need a cuddle from the supermarket. Or Eris!!!!!!!!

All is archived the same. Women do not exist for men's convenience. Is going off tech an inevitability? Œdipus killing Pops?

Woody approached Dagmar from the back. 'I'm worried about meeting new people,' he said. 'My nails are messy. I'm walking like a hot actor in a monster costume. Sweat is frisky my hair. Calm me down.' Dagmar sighed and got out a water bottle. Ten days later, Woody exercised a little bit, a not-Zeno amount, in a hemi-confident search of the hurt limit. No gym was needed for him. He was doing alright, like Ajax before the sword incident.

Dagmar told Orfeus that she needed a richer character. The author husly went on a quest of his own. Reading sucks, but writing is moreso. Dagmar has never demanded anything of Woody.

Film. Greysilver wheels, sectorial gaps between the spokes. Flammable in the open. Characterless, just frames. Observing. Not much happening. Seen by few.

Sprogs. Woody preparing. Gotta be sensible. Hide the booze.

+++ |+++++++++++++++
+++| ++
+++
+++
+++

Hopefully good will get through this. Redemption.

Let's now have a quiet giggle over foolish men. I'm more than a little excited about positive events.

"There is no death or threat in this book," said Dagmar.

In the beginning, as element 88 was discovered, a little girl named Dagmar was born. But I'm getting ahead of myself. This actual story begins earlier, in the realms of linear algebra, with one Dagmar getting to know mathsy material very well within her mother's uterus. All of this might actually be in *The Bismuth Quest*, a work written in one year. Some angular blobs are going to obscure the text in a moment!

…Plots exist for a reason.

Tendrils, vines, ships, jungles, betrayals.

e representation of the structure of bismuth?

es the point, said Woody happily as he coated th copious salt. I've been a fond eater since I Dagmar changed the universe by putting the ecade to get slim. Time's a fat thing at the mo, ther needed to listen to the downbeat bulletins either did. The sunny paradise of Kerno would

Anyway, on this particular day Woody could not find an old Bible. He listened to a Gregorian chant instead, on might have to com is Chance would be a

As an aside, Dag about cardigans. L

DAGMAR

You don't look disa

WOODY

I'm trying to keep a lid on me saucepan.

DAGMAR

There was a dullard in the cinema.

WOODY

That's ok. It was me. I was calculating the fifth derivative of a carving.

DAGMAR

I think the politicians have disabled hearts.

WOODY [musically]

The heart is not the only centre of the soul! I find my soul in my airways and majestic knees. Err, I think the politicos have disabled priorities.

DAGMAR [throwing a bare baguette like a javelin]

What's your morality, chum?

WOODY [whose computer is currently not working]

Biogenic.

DAGMAR

Drawn from the life?

WOODY [feeling helpless]

Yes, milady.

DAGMAR [thinking of the returning goddess]

What do you use your morality for?

WOODY [admiring the concept of practice]

Familial love. (…..) and defending the nation.

DAGMAR [hankering after bismuth]

Defending the nation's not your affair, Woody.

WOODY [after a long pause, one you could fit the *Ring Cycle* inside]

You're right. It's been a civil war between different groups of middle class people. I'm going to watch Eurovision.

DAGMAR

We are in 1849, sir.

Woody realised that he didn't have much in common with these weird people who wrote pamphlets, telegrams, notes and periodicals. Those people were so frustrating!

As an aide, Woody doesn't do chipwrapper crosswords because they involve sitting on yer batties too muč. He dashes about on this day, 16th of August 1849, in order to find his notes on zink [*sic*] and copper. He currently believes that his enemies are vainglorious; that is to say that vainglory is, in Woody's eyes, their chief sin.

Woody's not always so intense. Nine times out of ten you'll find a genial, pudding-filled man should you chance to meet him. He often pauses his strolls around the city in which he lives to admire Tudor beams. He loves rhomboid windows.

DAGMAR [thinking that things that can never go wrong can never be good]

We live in a vulgar age. I believe we need a gentle Christ.

WOODY [with the bravery of a falcon]

I, the hero, will tell you that we need open and empty parallel universes to deal with the troubles of tight lodgings.

DAGMAR

Do you feel moral?

WOODY [Thinks for a long time; then quickly] No, my dear, dear lady, I do not.

DAGMAR [with ambiguity and quite loudly]

How are your prayers, Woody?

WOODY [After a long pause; feel free to study the sky or scent the flowers]

Regretfully unanswered.

DAGMAR

Have you heard of Asaph Hall?

WOODY

No.

An interlude here on Woody's enemies; they might be of low intelligence, but Woody is of low fortitude and self-confidence. Woody's a trapped rat of a man. But, since solving the Riemann Hypothesis, he believes he's earned his lameness. Maybe he'll cheer up.

DAGMAR [holding *Pilgrim's Progress*]

Rise and walk.

WOODY

[…]

DAGMAR [putting her book down]

Have you heard of John Couch Adams?

WOODY [emphasising every word]

I have not.

DAGMAR

Urbain Le Verrier?

WOODY [politely]

N.

DAGMAR

Do you want to make Venus habitable, as a kindness to ladies?

WOODY

Yes. Many women are sly and battered, but I still care about them.

DAGMAR [baking two loaves]

Coarse sea salt, you are.

WOODY [putting his elbow in a sermon]

I'm an inveterate grumbler. I don't notice what others are doing. Right now, my trunk's a sack of potatoes.

DAGMAR [alone]

"There is" and "there be". Those are tough phrases to say and write.

WOODY [on *terra plus firma*]

My English is charmingly poor.

DAGMAR [compassionately]

Mr Redwood, why do you not cease from speaking about yourself?

WOODY [wishing he owned an imperial ton of bismuth]

Only person I know well. I respect the dignity of others by leaving them alone.

DAGMAR [scientifically, curtly]

You read the writings of itinerant, unhappy priests.

WOODY [lovingly]

Unhappy fools, who take no pride in their sufferings. We do not love what we display. When it comes to writing, one should respect one's leavings.

DAGMAR [with her knitted editor's cap on]

It's all in what we display, isn't it?

Woody replied that he had lost the thread. He felt like he was messing up, but not out of apathy. He sought out some unsightly cushions to throw and thump.

WOODY [in an accent from the north of the country]

I neglected me and mine in pursuit of a cold cause. I helped some peeps; maybe they're helping me now.

DAGMAR

This isn't a very nineteenth century novel.

WOODY [slowly]

Keeping the river.

DAGMAR

The one you mentioned?

WOODY [brisker now]

'Course. [Woody talks very quickly and agitatedly about the things that have wounded his awesome heart].

DAGMAR [in the press of answering emails and booking haircuts]

I'd better go.

By not spending forever on things, Woody managed to succeed calmly. His achievements were indelible. Slightly anachronistic clobber invited bits of sympathy towards him; Professor Redwood had no malign motive, but he wanted to be respected and ignored a little by other people. He's got long and strong arms that he uses to embrace his loves. I should have mentioned the details earlier, sorry. Tetra's the name of the village (now a village?) that this whole story is set in, by the way. It has some grey office blocks and a scary road – Blind Man's Bluff – where the wheeled armless crabs (some say 'motorcars') can come at you from all angles. It's all surreal nonsense anyway. Woody's asked me to put on the excellent local radio station and I will oblige.

WOODY [slightly pained]

I find it easier to communicate through the medium of prose.

DAGMAR

You put on your programme and then you quitted the room.

WOODY

I'm dealing with decay. And the evaporation of my time. Myself has quite enough to be getting on with without bringing in third parties.

DAGMAR [with dryness]

I don't have an expressive face. Silly violent rotters – it takes bones of steel to confront 'em.

WOODY [with a small amount of malice]

You try though, lovey.

DAGMAR

[as an aside] Not for you, Wood.

WOODY

Bickering. Bickering, eh? You make us seem rude, Orfa.

ORFEUS [peeling chewing gum off the stairs]

Go have one of your runs, Woody, you like those.

DAGMAR

[knocks]You wanted to see me?

ORFEUS

Yes. You are right to address me without styles, for I am your equal.

DAGMAR

You're just making this up as you go along, aren't you? [scoffs]

ORFEUS [to himself]

I wish I could be a zippy supernatural dragonfly, or a flying pair of eyeballs.

DAGMAR [hearing perfectly]

Why a pair of eyeballs?

ORFEUS

Depth perception.

DAGMAR [stomach growling]

Am I magma? The elites lost their nerve. A fabulous day.

ORFEUS

No.

DAGMAR [studying an acer]

Woody says you sense the eyeballs on your texts.

ORFEUS

He's wrong. And I can't say 'texts'.

[Another scene. The author got bored with that one].

WOODY [in a still churchyard]

My exams were a nightmare from which I'm trying to wake up. The modules became mosquitoes in my dippy hurricane of confusion. If I had been calmer I might have been able to organise myself better. But in the depths of my struggles I thought "one day, I can shape something out of this lonely mire that really matters." (…) I don't want to miss the woods for the trees.

ORFEUS [sitting on a not-incongruous tree stump]

It took a lot of bravery to say that.

WOODY [electronically]

Do you remember being middle-aged? All the work? Our current stage is perfumed foppery.

DAGMAR

I still am! Savants… No aggravating indulgences.

   Dagmar's carrying-out of the daily chores caused her to ponder on the lives of contemporary young adults. What could explain the elves' surge in support for the First Consul? Were the crashes and deprivations of industrial life rendering the youth of 1849 rather doolally? Would the youthful multitude benefit from carrying out mechanical taskwork?

Woody put his hat on a branch of the hatstand in a sweeping motion. This domestic life! This vast manor, physically related, like a wing, to Halberd's castle!

Woody's the kind of person you get fed up with.

ORFEUS [wanting a cider]

I, the narrator, swear to intrude no more. My English is poor and tight-cornered, trapping.

Woody resolved to continue the Victorian novel he was in. His sweetheart, Dagmar, is at the top of the stairs of Tyran Halberd's castle. It's a spiral staircase; a = rA. Wide steps for Woody's size tens. When we first met him, was he not interacting with a staircase. Cal Cutter, that assassin, attacked him with a balisong and lopped off one of his hands. Woody's forgiven that. Cal seeks redemption. O, redemption! The hardest and happiest of literary themes!

WOODY [making a realisation at last]

Who are you, unknown person? A fool? A scribbler? A grub?

ORFEUS

A man. Bit old, bit grumpy, telegraph not working. Dippy. Not a genius.

It's the year 2049. Woody, a precognitive dwarf, and Dagmar, a precognitive elf, foresee cars and the internet coming to the village of Tetra, in Kornwall. This story is taking place in Tetra.

WOODY

Grr. I am not 'appy. Too many wires in AI. Too many screws.

DAGMAR [with a banal heroism that is really very admirable and which makes the twenty-first century a liveable one]

I know screws well. Respect our dignity as creatures of ink, s'il vous plait.

ORFEUS

Shush, madam. I am in charge. Your anger, your vituperativeness needs to decay.

WOODY [snidely]

You write like you do because you can't write properly. Can't dip.

ORFEUS [sniffs]

It's a learning process. Takes time. I keep some of the rough bits in to encourage others.

Dagmar thought this was wonderfully public-spirited. Of course, much was missed out in this recount. A lot of stuff isn't observed or recorded or remembered. Woody wonders if he was able to imagine a functional tale in his head at all in the year 2030.

Woody asked me if it's all just blurry photographs to me and I said no.

DAGMAR

Do you ever let your sentences breathe? The true believers don't stop.

ORFEUS

On occasion.

WOODY [stronger than his anxiety]

Gazania Day?

ORFEUS

'Course. One always slows down for flowers. We need to seal leaks. [takes a deep breath]. I would like to apologise. I have been selfish. I cannot cope well with life. I am wilfully miserable at times. Sometimes I don't know what I've lost. Maybe the guvment is to blame. Maybe I'm just weak. I'm sorry and I hope this book is quietly pleasing and entertaining. Like my characters, I am aiming for psychic growth and a new window-box of phlox. [to self]. Did that make the cut?

The day sweated in a muggy way.

WOODY

These are all non-sequiturs. Toil for equilibrium, let alone progress.

DAGMAR

You use the word 'all' too much. And progress is evil.

WOODY [with finger on chin]

Who was it who said "To have all, one must give all"?

DAGMAR [unsure]

Catherine of Siena?

Woody sat down with Orfeus and offered him a rizlah, which Orfeus declined. What are you trying to do here, mate, asked Woody. Orfeus ate the leaves 'cos he didn't know how to smoke. I'm aiming for a 'big baggy monster', to use Henry James' phrase, began Orfeus. *The Zeroes* was meant to be a long twentieth century novel, *Feet* was an attempt at an eighteenth century novel and *The Bismuth Quest* is my attempt to write a nineteenth century-er. I regard the nineteenth century as the apogee of world literature, although I don't know if I'd have liked nineteenth century novels so much if I'd been around when they were new. The future weighs on me a bit. I want to let go but not be weightless. I suppose it's a question of practice. I'm trying to entertain, really. I want people to take in the beauty of plants and birds. I remember yellowhammers and woodpigeons and ferocious magpies in the long grass of my home town. I remember that town's lustrous concrete and its snobbery between north and south. I was a southerner. Orfeus looked at the time. Bother. The time's flown away from me. It often does. I worry about my lack of discernment.

Woody asked if he (Woody) and Dagmar were to love. Yep starcrossed, said the arranging author. I don't think you can get four hundred pages out of this, said Dagmar at high volume but not unkindly, who had heretofore been listening at the keyhole and now strolled into the pub snug. Woody and Dagmar brushed their hands together. Your book's locations make little sense, said Woody, to Orfeus. I'm trying to be topological, replied the author. Dagmar then asked if the quest for bismuth was a symbol...

Orfeus, the old man, talked about the past

It's a good thing we all memorised the citations, said Dagmar to her friends. Anyway, Woody. We've found each other.

As an aside, Dagmar looks lovely in yellow. Just wanted to say that -Woody. She smells of sweat and an English garden. Woody looks lovely in that shirt. The hairdresser's done his bob nice.

It's a Dickensian shuffle, really, thought Dagmar as she tidied away the plates and yawned discreetly. I've many branches of tasks to do. Unsympathetically, I look for the bismuth – which wasn't a symbol for love, it seems – sleep; dance a bit with my husband, Woody; and respire throughout. I'm not an awful gin-soaked palace, no, I have opinions. A social conscience. A domino of progress, that's me. Woody thinks my moods are elevated, just as they were during the riots of 'Eighty. Were they? Was I alive then? I'm an elf, a long-lived elf. An elf of longevity. Woody's a short elf. Anyway, we now have to make it *down* the tower, out of the castle, onto the benevolent green and black grass.

Woody concurred with most of this. In severe times he bowed his head. He has the gait and drive of an energetic gibbon. Cal, a nemesis, is often on the television, campaigning and being infuriatingly smug. A clever man who uses his brain for evil but who goes to the theatre alone.

One could guess a long list of physical properties for *The Bismuth Quest*, but it might be easier for the author to blurt things. The author, camp as Christmas, needs to get his hair cut. Woody's the author. Woody has told Dagmar more than once that everything's about entertainment. Not necessarily competition.

Woody's a man and he needs single sex spaces. Set things up w/o women.

Notes on Seagulls: large, burly, not much seen in Kornwall of late.

What to do while waiting: to be honest, nothing. Woody wants to make psychic progress.

The life of Woodrow Redwood: Birth at Bedfordshire; Cultivation at Somerset; Death at Devon

Woody says that (arrow up) isn't him.

Those Victorian novels, they move at hasty pace, says Dagmar. A lot happens in a few lines, added Woody, in agreement.

So much stuff to listen to! I am incompetent. I suck. I mumble. I've got twitchy legs, but that's because I'm anxious and neurotic. Can't know everything. Eating and sleeping well. Finding the right notes.

Dagmar forgot how to say 'finish' as she was talking about the chores she'd done.

Grief. Loss. Death. Dagmar doesn't have the energy to say what she feels about the loss. Her eyes ache in their sockets. That beloved violet dress seems so unhappy and so lost. A lot of her personality is painted in that dress.

*

GOING TO GO SOON. Sorry for the all caps! If only I could dance and sing unabashedly. Music hall greatness doesn't run in the family. Light and sadness. Orange beast through the window, probably a hot dusk. Hidden sadness. Woody – me – is bowing his head again. Making something of the moody motions.

Sleepier than demons. Seat probably too low. Makes Woody feel like an ungainly giant. His doppelganger son, Edgar, feels the same.

Slow. Humour. Insectoid toys made out of wood. A chance to use the verb 'to whittle'. Moulding a new building, a set, a farm, a hotel.

Scratchy writing on the page. Add your own scratches!

I met that wise woman Deborah, prates Woody. Impressive, matriarchal lady, bit of a judge. Liked my 'do.

Enduring. Enduring 'pain in the butt' Woody.

I called him 'a pain in the *behind*', corrected Dagmar. An airless story sapped the walls. And these were fell walls, dangerous walls, walls with Homeric greatness in them beyond comparison, in addition to mosquitoes and tractors.

Woody and Dagmar are doing all right.

Writing up the day's trifles.

Concatenate into paragraphs.

Grief saps concentration and productivity.

Needing some joy!

The chaos has gone wrong. Cause and effect and habits have been shaken up in the jar.

I'm chewing on a lot of flaming mustard seeds today! spat Woody to Zephyrus, Boreus, Eurus and the other one.

The suvven one? asked Dagmar.

The south of Ængland. Struggle. Sternness. Deprivation.

Kneeling on the hard floor of modern digital life. Woody is the convict and the jailer. Interned at his own pleasure (never joy). Our lovers don't begrudge the rich their rockets, they'd just like a cosy life as well. The quietness with which to think, and perhaps a bit of cake.

Novel-writing is a game of patience, Woody tells the author.

Dagmar has an esprit de corps, but not in a day-by-day chummy sense. She wants what's best for the species and she can be pretty cold towards her own family.

Selective and patient, that is Woody these days.

Energetic -- FRENETIC -- but in pursuit of something good.

Dagmar took a book of astrological symbols out of the library, but she didn't read it. Some of the planets had dogs on them and canals as well.

Woody's got a monkish life now, just writing his experimental books and eating focaccia.

Escaping first. Life's but a western. Oh, the cynicism of the damned!

Owls

Fed up some dry, pensive June

Floating, foraging, his far-seeing eyes scry

An amiably barn-bound doglegged thickgloved hand

Taking flight, he glides like cyder,

A tubby oval with wings, nut brown,

Elegant as air, sickle-clawed

Unflinching

And lands on the back of your hand

Sparrow, Deceased

Small bundle, tawny rock

Dotted with flies

On hard pavement

Stomach slashed by a feline.

The body is scooped up

And flung onto a bank

Of gravel and wooden scraps

Dead and quietly disposed. Farewell.

Art and Science: The Arch

As the words slot together like the bricks in the Parthenon

Dactyls rise, undercoated white with nectar, tragic, fluffed, sufficient, defensive.

We struggle earnestly for some nicer stuff. Maybe Mithras will give it to us.

The marble, sculpted wonder walls our days. Equations light the ways.

The painter's perfect painted finger touches and shoots electricity so, so strong

The volts stir the chambers of the heart to play it like a pipe organ. The sounds don't ruck.

The rubeous spheres, shook in a dungeon, or fermented,

Form a drink, the ichor of crafted, crushed apples

Abacus rosy taste for drinking, restraint, space's sink

Practical, not CGI'd. Our lives are thunderstruck.

Sleep: Sore Labour's Bath (ref. *Macbeth*)

What is it like

To be in the deep brook

Where quietness lives and healing powers scent the walls

And disturbances do not rattle the eaves

Of dormancy?

Stoically carrying on through splintered skies he goes 'til he falls
sideways

Into the astronaut's brutish mattress

Shapes of the body's hollow heartstrokes glaze the sand

His lambent life glows in life's long sleep without land

As Night's stars scorch the gentle blackness.

He wakes blearily, as if irked or sugared,

Wakefulness gores with its alert claws

But during this well-earned nap

The eye-studs are gold diamonds.

Dreams: Not Unalloyed Goods

Dream joyfully, said the young man, like a rite unsaid, yet bronzed

The world inside has flumes and giddy loves, slow pains

It can keep you or capture you or put violins in your head.

Dream waves refract for more possibilities

Foggy like the night.

On this restful earth of fantasies and lead

Whatever the haemoclysm jibbers, I'll dream until I'm dead.

In some eternal dark morning

The glaciers of Iceland shake,

Icy lumps of the earth quake,

Founts of magma spume awake,

And leave a silver memory in the dreamer's lake.

Mine of Love

A robust, ripe, rasping low sound rather like

Old Earth clearing her throat

Rattles me into liveliness;

I'm unfocused, clapped out,

But staying awake for you as you work the machine.

On small square tables with views of Rome

Your use of milk, beans and water forms the thick drink

That presses my buttons like a tailor.

The tart, tight taste of caffeinated syrup,

Chirpy and assured, ritzy, creamy, fresh

Makes the bubbles froth on the back of my teeth,

So, my heart beats faster, its beats quickened by the beans in the cup.

You've plunged us, hotly, into granules of Mixolydian love

Hot and dry close together, passion rising and falling,

A cafetière of fancy in too small a space.

Brown seeds pull me in inward,

Tamping the tambour of my heart,

My dad bod turned to dregs

As the minuscule grains

Bob about in Brownian motion,

The steaming water and milk catch the backs of our mouths

Like amorous tongues under pressure,

Like bitter crumbs in suspension.

Woody remarks that we lose something of ourselves when we love, even before the loss. Getting a ventricle or two torn out is part of the point. Actions are usually the proof of love.

Autumnal Sighs

Happy poetry for a happier time

When concrete didn't eat the rivers

And we weren't reduced to matchstick men in a furnace

When earth was civil and decent

(a non-existent age, to be sure)

The lands hummed like fearful rocks

But a tawny, happy, folky future

Is where I'd like to go

A seaside retreat near Tetra,

And return to the strings of synths

Rotating diorama

Zoetrope

Leading the horses up and down.

Fragility

Sand, I'll heat it

I'll make le grand geste

I'll wrestle bears for you

And keep you warm under canopies of stars

The winds blur our minds

And fire bursts the trees

I'll cross the skin of this fissile world

And hope you stay with me

P.S. Woody got the bismuth at last. Chix and Edgar are over the moon.

*

DAGMAR [airily]

Hell's got excellent pyrotechnics.

WOODY

[in incredible shock]

Why r u here, beloved Dag? oh my!

DAGMAR [remembering the meme war]

Wherever you go, sweetheart...

WOODY

Lots of healthy ravens here. That pleases me. [To Dagmar, awfully seriously] Don't look back.

DAGMAR

Did we die trying to escape Halberd's castle? Did we?

WOODY [as a psaltery begins to play]

Maybe I should jack it all in and drive across Wales shooting ghosts.

*

As she listened to Woody, her heart thumping, Dagmar headed in the direction of the tobacco jar and lit her pipe on a candle. Had she made any progress since marriage? Did they find the bismuth?

The utopia won't happen.

Love and courtship will do.

Woody reads aloud from the Acts of the Apostles.

***

'None shall expel us from the paradise Dagmar has created,' said Woody.

THE END

Printed in Dunstable, United Kingdom

66323587R00057